Fin Butler and the Hounds of Gabriel

PHILIP JANVIER

Bluebox & January

Bluebox & January
St Stephen's Rectory
Belle Vale Road
Gateacre
Liverpool L25 2PQ

First published in the UK by Bluebox & January

www.blueboxaudiovisual.com
blueboxandjanuary@blueboxaudiovisual.com

ISBN-13: 978-0993517730 (Paperback)

ISBN-10: 0993517730

Philip Janvier

DEDICATION

To Malcolm Leck, my oldest friend, and lover of
the Fin Butler Adventures

CONTENTS

INTRODUCTION

I am reliably informed that many people, both adults and children, find reading difficult and avoid picking up a book. A combination of a lack of time, practice and patience, means that many find books are confusing or boring. In writing this book, I wanted to challenge that assumption and show that reading books can be exciting.

Therefore, this novel is shorter than any of the other Fin Butler Adventure novels, it has been designed to be fast paced and easy to read. All the places Fin visits are real, though some have been exaggerated, or added to, for the sake of the story. Whether I have succeeded or not is up to you, but I enjoyed writing this romp across Wales.

This novel introduces two new characters, Sparrow and Skye Cairn. Sparrow is presented more fully, in a new series of books I am creating, The Reece Edwards Adventures, and Skye was inspired by a niece of a friend of mine. At one point in this story, we meet Lawrie, Jacob and Mike. These characters are based on real people, and their names are included following a charity auction at St Stephen's Parish Church, Gateacre, Liverpool. Thank you to their sponsors who paid for their names to be included in this book.

Philip Janvier – 23rd January 2018

ACKNOWLEDGMENTS

This novel would not have been possible without the support of many people. Therefore, I would like to thank the following: Shirley Cowan and Sandra Doore, who plough their way through all my manuscripts offering criticism, correction and encouragement. To Jane, who has endured without complaint endless discussions about Fin Butler and never ceased to be supportive. To Alma and Dave for always being there. To God who has given me the desire to write and who recognises me as the work in progress that I am.

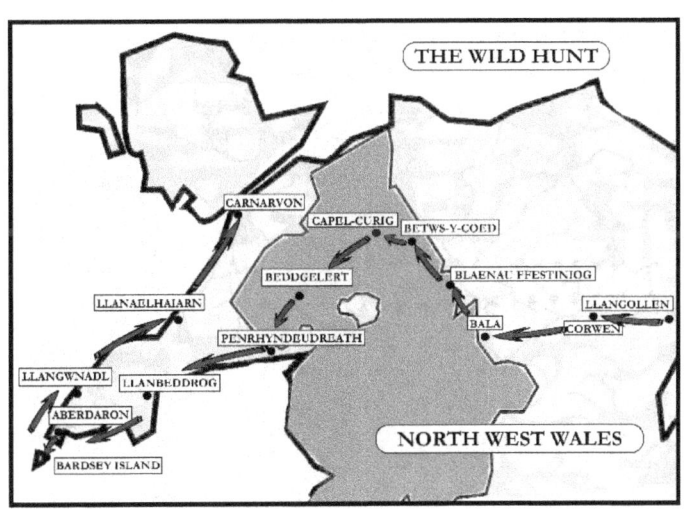

The Wild Hunt

North West Wales

OMEN OF THE NIMUË

I heard the cry of the Great Hound
I heard the sound of iron strike bronze
I held the living stone in my hand
And I heard Echidna's daughter scream in pain
I saw the Nimuë standing in the fog
I saw saliva fall from Gabriel's mouth
I saw the armlet of the missing one
And I knew that the Wild Hunt had begun
Ancient Fragment

CHAPTER 1 – THE WILD HUNT
(Llangollen)

'Whose stupid idea was this?' cried Jenny, as she pushed her wild hair away from her face, 'My hair is soaked, I am freezing cold, and my coat is not as waterproof as it once was.'

Thunder crashed, and lightning lit up the steep path in front of them. Rainwater flooded down the sharp pathway, making it treacherous underfoot.

'Yours,' replied Fin, 'I was all for admiring it, from down by the coach, but no, you insisted on climbing to the top. What was it you called me? "An ignorant, moronic, unromantic excuse for a boy."'

A strong crosswind whipped the rain into Jenny's face, and her reply was lost in the wind. Fin, however, seeing her face, interpreted the meaning and decided that now was not the time to push his luck.

'Well, we are at the castle now,' he continued, 'and we can shelter behind its walls.'

'A roof would be nice,' Jenny muttered, as she joined him behind the remains of one of the castle's walls.

The weather had been lovely down by the coach, and the prospect of climbing up to Castell Dinas Bran was irresistible. At first, being high above the Dee Valley and the town of Llangollen was breathtaking. However, as they approached the castle, a forty-mile an hour gust of wind had come out of nowhere and brought with it, torrential rain. The rain obscured all views of the valley below and with it, the warmth and shelter of Ravenswood's rickety old coach. Cuddling together, they tried keeping warm, but the wind and the rain made it impossible.

'Why did you want to come up here really?' asked Fin, as he tried to distract his mind from the rain.

'I sensed something bad was about to happen.'

'Something worse than being caught out here in a storm?' he replied.

'Yes, can't you sense it?'

Opening his mind to the environment around

him, Fin took in the hill the castle was standing on and let his mind wander. It was the perfect place to erect a fort, and the rugged pinnacle dominated the countryside.

'Nothing, I sense nothing at all.'

Despite Jenny's hair being rain-soaked, it seemed to take on a life of its own. While shorter than it used to be, it swirled in an unseen air and as it did, Fin began to gain a sense of foreboding. Jenny was seldom wrong about such things, and he had learned to trust her feelings with his life. Turning to face her, Fin looked into her eyes and waited.

A scream of pain permeated the hilltop, and as it did, a shiver ran down Fin's spine. It had come from inside the castle ruins. Suddenly it stopped, and his hands burst into flames. Someone was in trouble, in a flash; Fin Butler became the Phoenix, an extranatural guardian. A hand touched his arm, and Jenny shook her head.

'Let's find out what is happening first,' Jenny advised.

Nodding his head, Fin extinguished his flames and took Jenny's advice.

Quietly, they crept around the ruins until they found a gap in the wall. Standing in a circle, they watched twelve figures dressed in dark, hooded, cloaks surround, what looked like, a small, fourteen-year-old girl.

'Where is it, girl?' cried the figure nearest to her.

'I don't have it!' she replied.

Jenny held Fin back, as the figure slapped the girl across the face and she fell into the mud.

'Don't lie to me girl,' he said, as he dragged her

back to her feet by her hair. 'The Lord of Arawn sent me, and Lord Arawn knows... everything.'

Shaking off the figure's grip on her hair, the girl spat at his feet and cried, 'What makes you think that even if I had the "Magician's Stone," that I would just hand it over to you?'

'You are plucky, little girl, I like that,' the figure laughed, and then continued, 'but I am the Frân, and you are in my castle.'

'Not much of a castle,' she replied.

'But a good place to die... Give me the Sapphire or die, it is your choice.'

'Never!'

'Then you will die!'

'So you're the Frân,' said Sparrow, 'I wasn't frightened of the real Crow, so why should I be frightened of you?'

'You think you can defy me here, in Dinas Bran, Hill of the Crow?'

'I will defy you wherever I am!'

Moving menacingly, six figures stepped forward and picked up the girl. A seventh stretched her neck out, as the leader drew his sword and raised it into the air.

Horrified, Jenny's eyes turned black, and her hair stood on its end. Beside her, Fin transformed into the Phoenix, and they burst into the circle. Startled, the flock drew their swords and attempted to stop them. Trying to kill Jenny, two figures turned to stone as they swung their swords at her. Dropping the girl, the flock formed a circle around her. As the captive girl fell from their hands, she hit her head on a stone. As her consciousness faded, she wondered where the Gorgon and the Phoenix had come from.

~

Hiding in a gorse bush, they waited for the girl to wake up, while around them the flock searched the ruins.

Groaning, the girl sat up and spoke, 'Reece?'

'Who?' replied Jenny, as she stopped trying to clean a deep cut on her face.

'Not now,' whispered Fin, 'here let me.'

Nodding, Jenny let Fin use his Phoenix's powers to heal the wound.

'That should be better now,' continued Fin, 'but that's me out of power.'

'Who are you?' asked the girl.

'I am Fin Butler, and this is my friend, Jenny Cato.'

'The Phoenix and the Gorgon,' she replied.

'You saw that did you?' said Jenny.

'Yes,' the girl continued, 'you saved me.'

'And you are?' asked Fin.

'Sparrow.'

'Sparrow, is that all?'

'Just Sparrow,' she replied and then hearing the noise of the flock searching for them continued, 'I guess we are in a spot of trouble.'

A loud voice echoed around the hilltop, 'I know that you can hear me. I warn you that you cannot escape the Lord of Arawn's anger and you will burn in hell before he lets you escape with the "Magician's Stone".'

'Do you have the stone?' asked Fin.

Turning her eyes upon Fin and Jenny, Sparrow

wondered if she could trust them. Finally, making up her mind that she could, she replied, 'Yes.'

'Why do they want it?' he asked.

'It belongs to a friend of mine,' she replied, 'and it was taken from him by force. I want to return it to him and he would rather it was lost than give it to them.'

'Then it is a stone of power,' concluded Jenny.

'Yes,' replied Sparrow, 'and he needs it if he is to regain his powers.'

'What sort of powers?'

'He says it gives him insight, enlightenment and inner peace. It also has healing properties and gives him psychokinesis and telepathic abilities.'

'Hence its description as the "Magician's Stone."' added Fin. 'Then you keep it secret and safe we don't need to see it or hold it.'

'This is my final warning,' cried the Crow, 'hand over the stone now or die.'

Unwilling to reply they remained silent.

'Then you leave me no choice,' the voice paused and then cried out, 'Let the Wild Hunt begin... and the dogs will eat your bones.'

Overhead, thunder cracked, lightning lit up the landscape, and a dog's howl echoed around the hills.

OMEN OF THE NIMUË

Llyn Tegid	I HEARD THE CRY OF THE GREAT HOUND
Blaenau Ffestiniog	I HEARD THE SOUND OF IRON STRIKE BRONZE
Betws-y-Coed	I HELD THE LIVING STONE IN MY HAND
Capel-Curig	AND I HEARD ECHIDNA'S DAUGHTER SCREAM IN PAIN
Beddgelert	
Penrhyndeudraeth	I SAW THE NIMUË STANDING IN THE FOG
Llanbedrog	I SAW SALIVA FALL FROM GABRIEL'S MOUTH
Aberdaron	I SAW THE ARMLET OF THE MISSING ONE
Ynys Enlli	AND I KNEW THAT THE WILD HUNT HAD BEGUN
Llangwnadl	
Llanaelhaiarn	
Carnarvon	

CHAPTER 2 – GLYNDWR'S DAGGER
(Corwen)

Afraid to move, they lay in the shadows of the gorse bush until night fell and darkness dominated the hilltop. The rain had stopped but had been replaced with a moaning wind. In the distance, they could hear dogs barking and people shouting.

'How did you get here?' Fin asked Sparrow, curiosity getting the better of him.

'We were in Chester when we overheard a conversation in an old bookshop, and that made us think.' she replied, 'We had two options to consider,' shifting to get more comfortable, Sparrow hugged her knees to her chest, 'the sapphire was hidden either in Beeston Castle or here.'

Distant thunder echoed through the hills and valleys, and they huddled together for warmth.

'My friend had the blue stone taken from his armlet a long time ago.'

'How long ago?' asked Jenny.

'A long time...' Sparrow stopped and considered her reply, 'I best not say, you wouldn't believe me if I told you the truth.'

'You may be surprised,' replied Jenny, 'when?'

'It was taken from him in 1398 and handed to

Richard II.'

'Another time traveller,' snorted Fin.

'I told you, you wouldn't believe me!'

'Oh, we believe you all right,' said Fin, 'we've also been to another time and place.'

Lost for words, Sparrow stared at Fin.

'Ignore him,' interrupted Jenny, 'please finish your story.'

'Rumour has it, that Richard II hid the sapphire at Beeston before heading off to Ireland.'

'So why are you here?' asked Fin.

'We knew we were being followed, so I agreed to come here,' she replied, 'and try to get our watchers to follow me.'

'That obviously worked,' said Jenny.

'Too well,' continued Sparrow, 'because the stone was here at Dinas Bran.'

'I don't understand,' grumbled Fin.

'Wherever I led them,' she continued, 'had to be plausible, if unlikely. In Chester, we overheard a conversation that suggested, that this castle may be the burial place of King Arthur's "Holy Grail."'

The sky clouded over, and it began to rain.

'I didn't find the Holy Grail,' Sparrow said pulling up her hood, 'but hidden away from the wall I found the "Magician's Stone."'

'How?' asked Fin.

'My friend taught me the stone's name,' she added, 'so I called for it, and it responded with a bright blue light. Unfortunately, that's how the crows found me.'

'What did you do with the stone?' asked Jenny.

'I swallowed it.'

'Of course, you did,' said Fin, 'and how do you expect to get it out?'

Turning to face Fin, Jenny's eyes lit up, and she said, 'Do you really need her to answer that?'

'I will pass on that, thank you.'

'So will she,' laughed Jenny.

~

The persistent rain deadened any sounds of their pursuers and the wetter they became, the more miserable they felt.

'We can't stay here,' stated Fin, 'the colder we get, the worse off we will become. Let's head down the track to the car park and see what has happened to the coach.'

Quietly, they hugged the shadows and descended the hill. The coach was gone and in its place lay a muddy puddle with paw prints around it.

'You didn't really expect them to stay?' asked Jenny.

'No,' replied Fin, 'I was hoping that we might find Elizabeth and a search party.'

'Elizabeth knows we can handle ourselves, so she won't be worried yet.'

'Then we are on our own,' replied Fin, 'What do you suggest we do?'

'Head for Llangollen,' answered Sparrow, 'and try to get away from there.'

Agreeing with Sparrow, Fin and Jenny allowed her to lead them to the towpath of the Llangollen Canal.

~

Dawn arrived in a grey mist as they entered into Llangollen. Standing in the middle of the road bridge over the River Dee, stood two dark figures with dogs by their sides.

'This doesn't feel right,' Jenny said as she pulled them into a doorway.

Not inclined to argue, Fin led them down a path to the old railway station. As they hid in the shadows, a loud hissing announced the arrival of a steam train. Pulling up at the station, the laughing stoker and driver jumped down on to the platform and headed into the office. Unseen, Fin, Jenny and Sparrow moved up the platform, climbed into a carriage and sat down.

An hour later, they awoke to the rocking and clanking of a moving steam train. Looking out of the window Sparrow laughed. 'We've nearly travelled the full seven-and-half miles of the track,' she said, 'we need to be ready to get off.'

The train stopped. Unnoticed, they slipped out of the carriage and headed for a bus stop on the main road.

~

As the bus approached Corwen, Sparrow pulled out an envelope and opened it. Taking out a letter and a page torn out of a book she read the contents and went quiet.

'Are you okay?' asked Jenny.

'My friend told me to open it if anything went wrong,' she replied, 'Do you think this counts?'

'I guess so,' she answered, 'does your friend have a name?'

'It's complicated.'

'How complicated can a name be?'

Sighing to herself, Sparrow replied, 'He

introduced himself to me as Reece, but that's not his real name.' She paused and looked out of the window, 'We think we know his real name now, but he'll always be Reece to me.'

'Fair enough,' continued Jenny, 'Are you going to read the letter?'

'I already have,' she replied, 'here read it for yourself.'

Poking Fin in the side, she woke him up and together, they read the letter.

Hi, Sparrow,

If you are reading this, then something has gone wrong, and we are in trouble. In the bookshop, I found this poem slipped into an old book, and it reminded me of my quest. I don't believe it was there by chance, I think I was meant to find it. I believe that if we both follow it, we will meet up on the way.

Be safe.

Reece.'

'Interesting,' said Fin, 'but was Reece talking about the poem or the list of names written in green ink down the side?'

'I don't know,' she replied, 'it could be either or both.'

'It's a strange list,' Jenny said, holding the paper up to the bus window, 'some I recognise and some I do not.'

Fin attempted to read the list out aloud but struggled with the names.

In the seat in front of them, an old lady burst out laughing and turned around to face them,

'Would you like me to read those names?' she asked.

'Yes please!' exclaimed Sparrow.

'Llyn Tegid, Blaenau Ffestiniog, Betws-y-Coed, Capel-Curig, Beddgelert, Penrhyndeudreath, Llanbedrog, Aberdaron, Ynys Enlli, Llangwnadl, Llanaelhaiarn and Carnarvon.'

'Thank you,' said Sparrow, 'I recognise a few of them.'

'Well my cariad,' she continued, 'you being English I'm not surprised. Llyn Tegid is better known as Lake Bala. Penrhyndeudreath, you will have heard of because of Portmeirion.'

'Why would I know that?' whispered Fin to Jenny.

'"The Prisoner" was filmed there.'

'Never heard of it!'

'The Tin Man is at Llanbedrog, St Mary's Well is in Aberdaron, and Ynys Enlli is Bardsey Island.'

'I think we need to buy a map in Corwen,' observed Fin.

'It is a lovely list of places,' said the old lady, 'but some of them are a bit out of the way. Desolate you might say.'

'Thank you, you have been most helpful,' said Sparrow politely.

'I apologise for interfering,' continued the old lady, 'but I heard the hounds last night, and I recognise those names as part of the mystic's trail. I think that you are in trouble so I will try to help you.'

Stunned, Fin, Jenny and Sparrow sat in silence.

'If the hounds are chasing you, then you will

need the whistle and the dagger.' The old lady paused, 'I see that you have no idea what I am talking about. Bala is the home of King Arthur's faithful hound, and it is said, that if you blow the stone whistle, she will aid you.'

'And the dagger?' asked Fin.

'Glyndwr's dagger can be found here in this little town of Corwen.'

Her eyes closed Jenny put her hand in Fin's and said, 'She is telling the truth.'

'Why are you helping us?' continued Fin.

'I may be old, but I'm not stupid,' she replied, 'I have heard the hounds three times in my life, and after each time, bodies were found in the hills.' She paused, and a tear escaped from her eye, 'The last time I heard them, it was my son, Glen, who was found mauled to death.' Angrily, she wiped the tear away, 'I dare say, that many here see me as being mad.'

'Thank you,' replied Sparrow, 'Do you have any idea how we find the whistle and dagger?'

'I am sorry, I have never seen the dagger, and the whistle is well hidden. However, I will tell you what I know.'

~

Following the old lady's instructions, they left the town centre and headed for the mission church. As evening approached, a veil of mist came down and made their last few steps into the church grounds more difficult.

'Where did she say?' asked Jenny.

'Above the South porch,' replied Sparrow, 'you should be able to feel cross like grooves cut into the lintel.'

Stretching up, Fin ran his fingers through the grooves.

'Who disturbs Glyndwr's dagger?' cried a figure obscured by the evening fog.

An old photograph of Skye Cairn.

CHAPTER 3 - THE GREAT HOUND
(Bala)

'Flaming Norah,' cried Sparrow, as she turned to face the figure.

'Who disturbs Glyndwr's dagger?' repeated the voice.

Bursting into unexpected flames, Fin illuminated the porch and turned to face the figure. As the light cut through the mist, it revealed a small, dark-haired girl aged about twelve. Startled, she pulled down over her eyes a pair of aviator's goggles and stood defiantly staring at Fin.

'Is that supposed to impress me?' she asked, 'Because if it is, I have seen better tricks!'

Unable to stop himself, Fin burst out laughing and then Jenny started too.

'I thought you were the Nimuë,' said Jenny, when she finally gained control of her voice.

'Do I look like the Lady of the Lake?' replied the girl, as she pushed her goggles back up on to her forehead.

'No, not at all,' continued Jenny, 'but it's the sort of thing she would do.'

Bravely, the girl approached them, 'Why are you here?' she asked.

'It's a long story,' began Fin, 'and I'm not sure that now...'

Out of nowhere, a giant dog landed on the path and began to howl. Soon the night filled with the sounds of dogs barking.

'No time,' screamed the girl, jumping up and pulling the dagger out of the wall she cried. 'Run, I will handle this puppy!'

Gripping the dagger in her hand, she waved it in the air, and it pulsated with light. Howling in anger, the dog jumped at the girl. Before Fin, or the others, could react, the light from the dagger struck the dog on the snout, and it burst into flames. Howling now in agony, the creature tried to escape. Suddenly, it exploded into a cloud of dust and was gone.

'I thought I told you to run,' cried the girl, as she pushed them back down the path. 'I caught that one by surprise, next time we might not be so lucky.'

'Where to?' asked a breathless Sparrow.

'The village,' she replied, 'they are not strong enough to take us in a populated place,'

Running down the path, Fin introduced himself and the others, 'And you are?' he asked.

'Skye,' she replied, 'Skye Cairn.'

~

His sides aching with pain, Fin ran down Hill Street and pointed towards the bus stop. 'If we are quick we might be able to catch the last bus to Bala!' he yelled.

'Surely, we are too late,' cried a breathless Jenny.

Waving a timetable in the air, Fin replied, 'According to that clock, we've got a few minutes.'

As if on cue, the last bus arrived, and they jumped on and sat down.

~

Arriving late in Bala, they left the bus and walked down the High Street and turned off the main road into Cambrian Terrace. The street lights flickered and faded, casting shadows that seemed to move and follow them.

'The shadows give me the creeps,' said Sparrow.

'Because they are not shadows,' replied Jenny, 'the hounds have followed the bus to Bala.'

'What have you guys been doing,' whispered Skye, 'I've never known them to be so brave?'

'It's a long story,' replied Sparrow.

The lights continued to flicker and fade, and the shadows multiplied. Every now and then, twin red eyes would look in their direction and then blink out.

'It's no use,' said Fin, as he led them off the main street towards some stone cottages, 'we can't outrun them, we need to find somewhere safe to hide.'

'Good luck with that idea,' muttered Jenny, 'we are trapped in the dark.'

Quietly opening a sprung gate, Fin indicated that they should follow and they hid in the bushes of an untamed garden. A cat sitting on the stone step of the house continued to wash, oblivious or indifferent to the presence of the dogs that began to fill the narrow road. Lazily, it mewed and stretched.

Fascinated, Fin watched the cat stretch its limbs and then jump onto the stone gatepost. A gentle breeze whistled through a hole in the carved gatepost and with it came the stench of death.

'I told you that you could not hide,' said a voice from the shadows, 'now you are mine.

The tall, dark figure of the Frân walked to the gate and placed his hand on the latch. The cat jumped, and the man screamed as its claws dug into his face. The dogs howled, and more cats appeared from every corner of the garden and climbed onto the wall. The door to the house burst open, and light blazed out and illuminated the yard.

'Frightening young children again are you Frân?' said the old lady that they met on the bus earlier, 'You know better than to try to enter my property.'

'These children are mine,' he replied, 'and I want them now, Gwyneth.'

'They are under my protection.'

'Only while they are on your property,' sneered Frân.

'Then for this night they are safe, and you can resume your chase another day.'

'Lord Arawn, will be displeased.'

Gwyneth began to laugh and as she did so, the years fell away, and a woman of about thirty stood in the doorway.

'I have displeased Lord Arawn so often in the past, I am thrilled that I can still do it!' she replied.

Astounded, Fin watched Frân bow his head in grudging respect and walk away.

'Please come in,' said Gwyneth as she opened

the door wide, 'for you now have nothing to fear this night.'

~

Sitting around the kitchen table, hugging hot drinks to their chests they watched Gwyneth prepare them a meal.

'Are you a witch?' asked Sparrow.

'Heavens no, my dear,' she replied, 'I am no witch, nor devil, nor fallen angel. For I am Gwyneth Gwyniad, and I am extranaturally old.' She paused and looked closely at Fin, 'I sense that you too have the potential to live a long life, for I knew your Father before his powers faded. But even he was young compared to me. When I moved to this land, it was full of snow and ice. When it receded, there was a war between the birds, humans and the guardians. I alone survived and kept this place safe.'

'But I thought you lived in Corwen,' said Skye, interrupting Gwyneth's explanation.

Laughing again Gwyneth replied, 'I do sometimes live there, I like to know that the dagger is being looked after. And don't give me that look Skye Cairn, for I knew your mother, and she had the same look.'

'I named the lake, "Llyn Tegid" - Lake of Serenity. I remember them building King Tegid's Palace, and I watched it drown.'

'Did you know King Arthur?' asked Skye.

'Indeed I did,' she replied, 'in the 6th Century he used to gallivant around here.'

'What was he like?' asked Fin.

'As a young man he was fun, and we played

together,' she laughed, and its sound rippled in the air, 'He even had a nickname for me! But he changed, he grew sick of this backwater and began to desire power. Only my old friend Merlin could calm his excesses and only then at the price of their friendship.'

Interested, Fin gazed into Gwyneth's eyes and saw that she was both young and old, that she knew love and laughter but that there were no shadows there.

'I think I know who you are,' said Fin and then quietly wolf-whistled.

Shocked, Jenny poked Fin in the side and told him to behave.

A smile of understanding crossed Gwyneth's face.

'So Merlin existed too,' said Sparrow.

'And still does,' she replied.

Turning to Fin, Jenny asked, 'Why did you wolf-whistle?'

'Because,' said Fin, 'Gwyneth and Arthur were a couple once and he used to whistle like that at her.'

'You mean that Gwyneth, is the Great Hound of King Arthur,' said a confused Jenny. 'I don't understand!'

'It has been lost in translation,' said Gwyneth, 'and it amuses me not to correct it.'

Understanding crossed Jenny's face, 'When you broke up, he got so angry with you that he called you a big bitch!'

Gwyneth - 1901

CHAPTER 4 - SALIVA
(Bala - Blaenau Ffestiniog)

Fin tossed and turned in his sleep, something was missing, and he could not find it. Stumbling over a rock in his dreams he awoke, to see he had kicked the wall. Around him on the floor, the others slept on borrowed cushions and blankets. Outside the house he could hear dogs howling but felt no fear, Gwyneth's protection in her own home was absolute. Sitting up, he glanced around the room and noticed Gwyneth staring out of the window into the night.

'It is many a year since something has stirred the hounds like this,' she said without looking at Fin, 'and if they have woken Gabriel, then I fear for you.'

'Gabriel, I thought he was an angel?'

'Oh, how I wish he were that Gabriel,' she sighed, 'it is many a year since I have seen his beauty.'

'You've met an angel,' said Fin, 'I thought they

were rarely seen outside the bible?'

'Gabriel, is a messenger,' she replied, 'and many have met angels without knowing it. He once asked me to do something for him, and I was thrilled to do it.'

'Was he scary?'

'He was both terrifying and beautiful at the same time. The second he spoke, I felt so unclean... unworthy. But he just told me not to be afraid and then asked me to pass on a message to...' Falling silent, Gwyneth turned to face Fin and blushing said, 'The message was so private it's best I say no more.'

'If the Gabriel you are referring to is not an angel, who or what is he?' asked Fin.

'The leader of the Wild Hunt,' she replied, 'The hounds of Annwn are an experiment gone wrong, to some they appear as swans or geese, to others dogs. They adapt their form for whoever they are chasing, and they never give up.'

A howl filled the air and Fin shivered.

'You need not fear them while they howl,' continued Gwyneth, 'for they only howl when they are distant from their prey. It is when they go quiet that you are in trouble.'

Unable to help himself, Fin yawned, and Gwyneth told him to sleep. Unable to stay awake he fell into a deep sleep.

~

Bright light streamed through the window, and it took Fin a while, to remember that he was in Bala being chased by the hounds of Gabriel. His unpleasant thoughts were disturbed by the smell of fresh coffee brewing. He jumped up and went into the kitchen. He hadn't noticed the night before how beautiful Gwyneth's house was. Every surface gleamed, and the kitchen looked like it had been made for a traditional Welsh museum.

'Coffee?'

'Yes please,' he replied and then taking the offered cup he sat down.

'I've been thinking,' said Gwyneth, 'we need to get you out of Wales before the hounds of hell catch you. But you can't go back to England via Llangollen, that's too obvious.'

Bringing her coffee cup with her, she sat down next to Fin and smiled.

'I will escort you as far as I can, but I'm not sure how far that will be. As I get older, my powers become a little inconsistent, and I may end up being more of a liability than a help. However, I think that it would be best if we keep you to the tourist routes and try to get you to North Wales.'

'Won't that put other people in harm's way?'

'I don't think so. The hounds rarely attack their prey in front of people, that's not how they work.'

Nodding his head, Fin agreed and asked, 'Where should we head for?'

'I think we need to head for Betws-y-Coed and then Conway,' she replied. 'From there you can get a train to Chester and then to Crewe.'

'How far can you travel with us?'

'I've no idea, it has been a long time since I left these hills.'

~

Moments later, the kitchen filled with noise and

bustle as the others woke up and joined them.

'You're coming with us?' cried Jenny in excitement.

'Yes I am,' replied Gwyneth, 'but I'm not sure how far I can travel with you, but I would love to see Betws-y-Coed again.'

Only Sparrow seemed unimpressed.

'Are you feeling okay?' asked Jenny.

'Not at all,' replied Sparrow, 'I have stomach cramps, and I'm constipated.'

'Is it?' began Jenny.

'Not for a couple of weeks, this feels different.'

Overhearing the conversation, Fin leaned over and said, 'You swallowed a gemstone maybe it's got stuck.'

'Crap,' replied Sparrow, 'in all the excitement of the chase, I'd forgotten that.'

Groaning in agony as the stomach cramps overwhelmed her, Sparrow turned grey and fell to the floor in pain.

'What is it?' asked Gwyneth, as she knelt down next to Sparrow.

'She swallowed a gemstone, rather than let the Frân have it.'

'If it sticks we will need to get her to a hospital,' said Gwyneth, 'I've seen this before when a friend's son swallowed a penny.'

Standing up Gwyneth, helped Sparrow out of the kitchen and lay her down on an old sofa.

'If she gets any worse I'm calling an ambulance.'

'What about Frân and the hounds of Gabriel?' asked Jenny.

'One emergency at a time,' she replied, 'but one

thing is for certain, we are not going anywhere today.'

'Maybe I can help,' said Fin.

'How?' asked Gwyneth.

'Fin, as the Phoenix, has healing powers,' replied Jenny, then added dubiously, 'but this is quite different...'

Placing his hands on Sparrow's head, Fin closed his eyes and concentrated. His hands began to glow and his face contorted in pain. Sparrow's eyes opened wide, and she screamed.

Falling backwards, Fin fell into Jenny's arms as Sparrow jumped up, ran out of the room and into the toilet.

'Was that supposed to happen?' asked Skye, 'Because I'm not so sure...'

'I'll check,' said Jenny and left the room.

~

Half-an-hour later, Jenny and Sparrow rejoined the others. Colour had returned to Sparrow's face, but Jenny looked slightly green.

'Well,' began Sparrow, 'I know who my friends are.'

Sitting Jenny next to the open fire, Fin sat down next to her, 'Are you okay?' he asked.

Unable to reply, Jenny started laughing and held out her hand. As her fingers opened, blue light emitted from the gemstone in her hand.

'Wow,' cried Skye, 'the stone came out!'

'It came out alright,' said Sparrow, 'I think it's fair to say that I am not constipated anymore.'

'How did you find it?' continued Skye.

'I didn't,' she replied, 'I was in too much pain...

Jenny did.'

Unable to help himself, Fin started to laugh, 'You poked around in Sparrow's poo until you found it?'

'It wasn't poo...' Jenny replied, 'and yes, we didn't dare flush it away.'

Pausing, Fin realised that he was holding Jenny's hand and suddenly let go.

'I have washed my hands,' she said indignantly.

However, no one was listening to her reply, they were all too busy laughing.

~

The following morning, Gwyneth ordered a five-seater taxi, and once it had arrived, they all jumped in.

'This is an obvious way of leaving Bala,' she explained, 'but the Frân will be watching us, so there is no point trying to sneak away.'

'Which way would you like to go?' asked the driver.

'Efrydan Road and via the A4212,' Gwyneth replied.

'Gazing out the window, Fin enjoyed the route through Frongoch and into the hills.

Forty minutes later, they arrived at Blaenau Ffestiniog and entered the Railway Station.

'What's that up there?' asked Skye, pointing up at the shape of giant dog up on the hill opposite.

As Fin stared at the dog, large dollops of saliva dripped from its mouth, and it howled.

Placing her arm on Fin's shoulder, Gwyneth whispered into his ear, 'That is Gabriel, the leader of the hounds of hell.'

CHAPTER 5 - THE SLATE MINES
(Blaenau Ffestiniog)

The wind blew coldly up the valley, and they all shivered as they stood on the platform.

'It is as I feared,' said Gwyneth, 'the last time I saw Gabriel, someone... my son died.'

'Then you are afraid of him,' said Skye.

'No, not of him,' she replied, 'he can no longer harm me, I have served my sentence.'

'And your son?'

'My son became evil and murdered many people when challenged he refused to repent. So the hound hunted and killed Glen as an act of justice, or least Lord Arawn's version of it.'

The wind howled through the station and the afternoon turned cold.

'When was this?' asked Fin.

'A long time ago, when I used a different name.'

A steam train hooted and clanked its way down the track towards them. Stopping at the water tower, it's engineers jumped off and proceeded to fill its tanks with water.

'Who were you then?' asked Jenny.

'If I tell you, I may lose your trust,' she replied, 'but then, maybe if I do not, I will lose it anyway.'

'We judge nobody by their name or their family,' said Fin, 'by our actions, we are defined, and you have proved trustworthy. Therefore, the choice is yours, whichever, I consider you a friend.'

'Before I was Gwyneth, I was Scylla, the last daughter of Ekhidna.'

'The Mother of all Monsters,' said Skye, 'no wonder you are old, for you are immortal.'

'Scylla,' exclaimed Jenny, 'sometimes called Cato?'

'Indeed,' she replied, 'you know your mythology.'

'I know my family's!' she said, as her hair swirled in the air and her eyes turned black, 'For I am Jenny Cato, a descendant of the Gorgons, and you are my oldest living relative!'

The sound of laughter echoed through the hills, at its sound the hound of hell jumped down from its vantage point and vanished.

When the laughter subsided, Fin asked the question they were all thinking, 'Why did you change your name?'

'Skye called my mother, Ekhidna, the Mother of Monsters, and she was correct,' she replied, 'My sisters all did things I was ashamed of, and I tried to avoid them. But they sought me out, and we argued.' Gwyneth paused and wiped a tear from her eye. 'In those days, I could turn into a dragon...'

'Have you met my mother?' asked Fin.

'Was she a dragon too?'

Unable to reply, Fin nodded his head.

'Then maybe we all have more in common than I thought,' she said, 'I was a mighty dragon, with the head and body of a woman and the tail of a snake. When angered I could breathe fire and rot the earth with a look. I was fire and blight, and my anger was terrible. My sisters and I fought, the humans around us tried to hide, and many were killed. When the battle was over, a village was destroyed. I was devastated, I had tried so hard not to be a monster and still ended up killing people.'

Pain filled Jenny's eyes, and Fin took hold of her hand, 'Some of the Flock tried to kill us, and in defending ourselves, we have killed people too,' he said sadly.

'I tried to hide,' she continued, 'so I came to this land with a desire to be different. I changed my name, and my new name became a blessing rather than a curse.'

'And Glen?' said Jenny prodding.

'Glen was the son of King Arthur and me,' she replied, 'a beautiful child who turned into a monster. He killed and tortured people for pleasure, all he was interested in was power and politics.'

'What happened to him?' asked Skye.

Gwyneth paused and stared into the past, 'The Archangel Gabriel visited me with an ultimatum to pass on to my son. He told me that I was forgiven and that Glen could be too.'

'Let me guess,' continued Fin, 'Glen could only be forgiven, if he stopped what he was doing and changed direction, in the way that you did.'

'As instructed by Gabriel, I delivered the message, and he spat in my face,' she said, 'For Arthur, that was the last straw, and he commanded Lord Arawn to chase him down and kill him. Until this point, Arawn and Arthur had been, if not enemies, then certainly bitter rivals. The great hound, renamed himself, Gabriel, to spite me and hunted Glen down, found him and killed him. Arthur and Arawn became great friends from then on, and Arthur changed, in my opinion, for the worse. We argued bitterly, and he left for Avalon, vowing never to come back.'

Suddenly, the platform was filled with steam and smoke as the old engine lumbered into the platform.

'Now,' cried Gwyneth as she pulled them into the shelter of the buildings, 'we hide.'

'I don't understand,' said Fin, as he was bundled into dark side-room.

'Gabriel has been watching us,' she replied, 'and he thinks we got onto the train. We will wait an hour, and then we go cross-country.'

'How?' asked Skye, 'As soon as they realise their mistake, they will be after us.'

'Gabriel is overconfident in hunting his prey down,' she replied, 'Once he realises his mistake, he will search the roads first.'

~

Struggling up the hill to the mine entrance, Fin mentally questioned Gwyneth's confidence, but he could think of no other possibility. Quietly, they entered the Llechwedd Slate Caverns by a side passage and stopped at an old shed.

'You will need these,' Gwyneth said, as she gave them helmets with lamps on them. 'The ceilings are low, and you will crash your head many times until we come out the other side.'

At first, they walked down a few public passages and then they entered a minor cavern.

'Do you want more light?' Fin asked.

'Not yet,' she replied, 'save your energy for it has been many years since I came down here and we may have need of it. Anyway, we are taking the train.'

'You're kidding!' exclaimed Fin.

'Stay here and wait,' she indicated that they should be quiet. Standing in the shadows, they heard a group of visitors approach them.

'You will be amazed by what a group of men, a candle and gunpowder can do,' the guide said, 'The deep mine you are about to enter, is accessible only by this narrow gauge and it is the steepest passenger railway in the United Kingdom. We will not be visiting all sixteen floors, but you will discover the appalling conditions the Victorian miner had to endure. Please take your seats.'

Climbing into the rear carriage, Gwyneth encouraged them all to take a seat. Once their descent began and the noise of the train was too loud for them to be overheard, she said. We will enter a cavern, and they will turn all the lights out. When they do, hold hands and stay close to me.'

'Won't they miss us?' asked Fin.

'The visitors were counted in from the ticket office,' she replied, 'as they don't know we are here, they will not miss us.'

'You've done this before,' said Fin.

'Possibly,' she replied, 'it once seemed a good idea at the time.'

The train trundled to a halt, and the lights went out. Ignoring the instructions of the guide to stay where they were, Gwyneth led them out into the darkness.

'We wait here,' she said.

Moments later the lights came on, and the voice of an ancient miner began to tell the visitors his story.

When the voice had finished the train clunked and clanked its way out of the cavern, and the darkness regained its natural hold over the rocks. In the silence, Fin began to wonder what they were letting themselves in for.

CHAPTER 6 - EKHIDNA'S RING
(Blaenau Ffestiniog-Dolwyddelan)

'Okay, you can put your lights on now,' said Gwyneth, 'we are out of sight here.'

'How far do we have to travel?' asked Jenny.

'If we were above ground and following a normal road, we should be in Dolwyddelan in just less than two hours,' she replied, paused and noticed that Jenny had not put her light on.

Smiling Jenny explained, 'I can see in the dark with my hair, and I'd rather save my light in case of an emergency.'

'That's a good point,' acknowledged Skye, 'we only need to use half our lights.'

Adjusting to a little less light and cracking his helmet on the ceiling, Fin envied Jenny's ability to see in the dark.

~

The route through the caverns was complicated, and occasionally they had to stop, while Gwyneth contemplated the way. Having never been underground before, Fin was amazed by the variety of caverns they travelled through. Some were large, with massive rocks hanging from the ceiling, others were vast underground lakes with rusty walls, but the most frustrating was the low tunnels in which he kept hitting his helmet on the roof.

Pausing again, Gwyneth sat on a rock and stared at a crossroad of tunnels.

'I don't remember any of this,' she said, 'and I can't see across the caverns.'

'What are you looking for?' asked Fin as Jenny came and held his hand.

'I remember a vast cavern, with a high up exit, but these are all flooded.'

'I can see something, creeping up the tunnel towards us,' said Jenny, 'it looks like oil.'

'What?' said Gwyneth, 'Where?'

Jenny pointed down the tunnel they had just walked up.

'I can't see anything?'

'Allow me,' said Fin, bursting into flames.

Immediately, they could all see a tide of water approaching them.

'It must have started raining,' began Sparrow.

'More like a deluge,' interrupted Skye,' that water is rising fast!'

'I know where we are,' cried Gwyneth, 'Fin, light up this cavern.'

Running into the open space, Fin illuminated the cavern, and Gwyneth pointed high up into a far corner.

'That's the only way out,' she said, 'but last time I was here, there was no lake.'

'Well there certainly is now,' replied Jenny, 'and the water is rising fast.'

'Everyone, put your lights on,' instructed Gwyneth, 'and climb up the walls to that outcrop.'

Water poured into the cavern and soon the tunnel they had come in by, was flooded. The climb was not challenging, but handholds would suddenly give way, and they would be left scrambling to safety. The outcrop once reached turned out to be a narrow and treacherous path around the edge of the cavern. Once more, they held hands and edged their way towards the exit.

'What's that?' asked Skye pointing into a space in the wall.

Entering carefully, Fin cast his light around the cave and saw the item that had caught Skye's attention. Protruding from an old cloth bag, was a broken sword with a gem-laden grip. Reaching out to pick the sword up, he touched the bag, and it disintegrated, leaving a skeleton hand still gripping the sword. On its finger, hung a tarnished gold ring.

'What is it?' asked Gwyneth pushing into the cave.

'The reason you searched these caverns,' replied Fin with unexpected understanding. Carefully, he removed the ring from the finger and placed it into Gwyneth's hand. 'Your son's I believe.'

Astounded, Jenny accidentally read Gwyneth's mind, 'You never found his body after Gabriel killed him.'

Gwyneth shook her head, tears glistened in her eyes.

'The ring was your mother's and the sword,

Merlin's.'

'You are reading my mind,' said Gwyneth, 'how dare you!'

'It's more that you are broadcasting yours,' replied Jenny, hoping no-one could see her blush in the dark.

'Sorry,' said Gwyneth, 'you are correct, I apologise for snapping at you. The ring was my mother's, and I did want it back, as it was all I had left of her.'

'You say the sword was Merlin's,' said Sparrow turning it in her hands, 'I would have imagined it would have survived the years better.'

'Its power was in its gemstones,' she replied, 'and by the look of it, only one of the originals is still in it. Please, will you look after it for me and if anything happens to me, ensure Merlin gets this back.'

'Merlin is still alive...' exclaimed Skye, 'How, it was so long ago?'

'And yet I am still alive...'

Water washed over the ledge and wet their feet.

'I'm not sure we were meant to find these,' cried Jenny, 'I sense a new... no, an ancient will... and it does not want us to leave these caverns alive.'

'Then we run,' cried Gwyneth, pushing her way out of the cave, 'follow me if you want to live.'

The scramble to safety quickly became a race against the rising water. Pathways became slippery, and the cold deadened their toes. Finally, they reached the exit, only to find the path destroyed and a large hole blocking their way.

'We will have to jump,' said Fin.

'I can't jump that far,' replied Skye.

'But I can throw you,' said Gwyneth, 'Fin, you or Jenny go first.'

'I will go first,' said Jenny.

Calmly, she took a short run up and without looking back ran and jumped the gap. Gravel scattered everywhere, but she was across.

'Fin, you next.'

Not as confidently as Jenny, Fin ran at the gap and jumped. Landing on the far side, he slipped and grazed his knee. Trousers ripped and his knee bloody he indicated that Sparrow should go next. With hardly any effort at all, Sparrow jumped the gap and landed gracefully on her feet.

'I was always good at the long-jump,' she said laughing,

'Your turn now,' said Gwyneth leading Skye to the hole.

Water continued to rise, and soon the lower part of the path was submerged. Apprehensively, Skye allowed Gwyneth to run alongside her. As the hole approached, Gwyneth threw Skye into the air, and she sailed across the divide. Unable to stop herself, Gwyneth slid over the edge and started to fall. Scrambling against her own momentum, she hung on a rock and crashed into the side, her feet hitting the turbulent water.

Groaning, Gwyneth climbed back up onto the path, limping she walked again ready to take a running jump. As she turned, Fin saw the angle of her arm and realised that it was broken. Sprinting as best she could, Gwyneth slipped as she jumped at the gap and fell short.

Transforming into the Phoenix, Fin leapt back over the gap and caught Gwyneth in midair. Landing in water, his feet turned the liquid into steam, and all visibility vanished in the mist.

'Fin!' cried Jenny unable to see what had become of them.

'It's okay,' he replied, as he appeared next to Jenny, still holding Gwyneth up, 'we are here.'

The walk up the cavern was eased by a steady flow of fresh air that flowed towards them. Soon they reached the surface to find their way blocked by a welded iron lattice.

'One last obstacle,' groaned Gwyneth, 'they've blocked the way off to stop people coming down here.'

'That's no problem for me,' said Fin, as he gripped the ironwork in his hands. Moments, later he pushed the way open, helped them all out and resealed the entrance.

'Just one last thing to do,' Fin continued and looking at Gwyneth said, 'This is going to hurt.'

'I'm not afraid of pain,' replied Gwyneth.

'But I am,' said Fin as he enveloped her as the Phoenix and screamed in agony as he healed her of her injuries.

CHAPTER 7 - THE TEA SHOP
(Betws-y-coed)

Emerging above Dolwyddelan, they made their way, as best they could, down the hill. The earlier rain had converted the footpaths into overlapping streams. The descent was tricky, but fortunately not impossible.

'All this water does mean that hounds will have difficulty picking up our scent,' said Gwyneth.

'True,' muttered Jenny, 'but my feet are freezing.'

Nevertheless, they arrived safely in the picturesque village and waited on the bridge, while Gwyneth and Jenny organised transport.

'That was amazing,' said Gwyneth, as she called the others over to the bicycle shop, 'the owner wasn't keen on lending us the bikes, but Jenny just smiled at him and asked him again. I think he was as surprised as we were that he said yes.'

Before Fin could speak, Jenny jumped in, 'Yes I gave him the eye. And yes, we are paying for them, and we agreed the extra insurance in case anything happens to us.'

'The eye?' said Gwyneth.

'Oh come on,' replied Jenny, 'I am, after all, one of your descendants. As well as turning people to stone, I can occasionally get them to do what I want.'

'Occasionally?' spluttered Fin.

'I can't do that,' said Gwyneth.

'I think we should collect the bikes before the owner changes his mind,' said Fin interrupting, 'Maybe you can explain on the road when we have more time.

Moments later, they were cycling along the main road towards Betws-y-Coed.

~

The thirty-minute journey was uneventful, and they soon arrived, hot and sweaty, in the town. Unable to avoid the A5 and after a couple of near misses, they parked their bikes next to the first tea shop that took their fancy. Unable to pronounce its name, Fin smiled and entered Cafi Caban-Y-Pair and sat down. Glad to be off the main road the others quickly joined him.

'I hadn't realised how hungry I was,' he said, 'until I saw that specials board.'

Laughing, Jenny read it out aloud, 'Tomato and Basil Bruschetta, Insalata Caprese, Pork and Beef Meatballs, Pork and Fennel Meatballs and Roasted Goat's Cheese with Bruschetta... Yum, yum!'

'I wasn't planning a long stop,' said Gwyneth, but seeing the disappointment cross their faces, agreed to stop for lunch.

~

An hour and a half later, Fin disgraced himself by burping loudly, but no one cared. That is until Gwyneth looked out the window and saw a large German Shepherd looking in at them.

Looking up, Jenny glanced into the dog's eyes and screamed in pain. Holding her head in her hands, she whispered, 'That dog is the first, but the others are on their way.'

'How long?' asked Fin.

'Don't know,' she replied, 'but I sense that the others had headed towards Conway, and he's been left behind just in case they'd missed us.'

'Then that route has been cut off for us,' groaned Sparrow.

'Then we take the bikes and head towards Beddgelert,' said Skye, 'it will give us a head start.'

'But how do we leave here, without it following us?' asked Fin.

'You pay the bill,' said Jenny to Fin, 'and I'll have a word with it.'

'Be careful,' Gwyneth said, 'that's not a normal dog.'

'And I'm not a normal girl,' she replied.

'And that's the truth,' said Fin.

'I'll pay,' said Gwyneth, 'you watch Jenny's back.'

Nodding in agreement, Fin followed Jenny to the door and slipped outside.

Kneeling down in front of the dog, Jenny stared into its eyes and fell silent. To anyone passing by, it seemed as if she was making friends with the dog. However, Fin could see a drop of perspiration drip down her face. Walking over he knelt down next to her and put his hand on her shoulder.

Instantly, he was in a dream-state, and the dog was talking.

'Foolish girl, did you think your puny powers could control a hound of Gabriel?'

'It was worth a try.'

'A waste of energy, for I am beyond your mind control.'

'Indeed,' she replied, 'but I can do more than that.'

'You could try turning me to stone, but as I don't exist in material form, it will fail.'

'Shame, but you still underestimate me.'

'How? One little girl is no threat to me.'

'I agree,' she said, 'but there are two of us here, and while I can't kill you, we can send you back to where you came from.'

Grabbing hold of Fin's hand, Jenny's eyes went black, and her hair swirled. Beside her, Fin burst into flames and poured fire on to the shocked animal. Unable to deal with two threats at once, it disintegrated and vanished.

Opening his eyes, Fin squeezed Jenny's hand, and they returned to the tea shop.

'Well done,' said Gwyneth, 'I've no idea what you have done, but it is time to get out of here before its friends return in numbers.'

Jumping up Skye headed for the toilets, 'Sorry,' she cried I need the loo.'

'We'll meet you by the bikes,' replied Jenny as she led Fin out the door.

While the others waited for Skye, Fin and Jenny began to unlock the bikes.

'How long do you reckon it will take Gabriel to find us?' asked Jenny.

'No time at all,' growled Gabriel, as a giant hound appeared beside them and licked their faces.

Instantly, Fin and Jenny collapsed to the ground as their limbs failed to respond to their desire to flee. Feeling sleepy, Fin realised there was nothing he could do as he watched Gabriel lean over him and lick him again.

'No one escapes me,' Gabriel whispered, 'and I was so hoping for a challenge this time.'

His conscious mind drifting away Fin watched two young boys run around the corner and spot Gabriel licking him. Excitement filled their faces, totally unaware of the danger they were in they approached Gabriel and began to stroke him. To Fin's surprise, Gabriel rolled over and allowed them to tickle his tummy. Seemingly oblivious to Fin and Jenny, Gabriel whined as if enjoying the attention. Clarity began to return to Fin's mind, and he found that he had movement again. Bumping into Jenny, Fin realised that she too was regaining the use of her limbs. Pulling themselves up they stood next to their bikes as Gwyneth, Sparrow and Skye exited the tea shop.

Quickly assessing the scene, Gwyneth finished unlocking the bikes and urged Sparrow and Skye to head off immediately. 'Come on,' she said as she helped Fin and Jenny onto their bikes. 'Gabriel is helpless around innocents, he has no power over them and cannot hurt you in their presence. You were lucky he tried to take you in a public place.'

Climbing onto their bikes, they cycled off up the

road and away from the danger. Stopping for a moment, Fin looked back and saw two adults approach the children.

'Daddy,' cried one of the boys, 'we've made a friend!'

'Lawrie,' he replied, 'you and Jacob have to be so careful, you can't just go up to strange dogs and start playing with them.'

'But they were playing with two of those teenagers we saw through the window of the tea shop,' said Lawrie.

'The dog was licking them,' added Jacob, 'and seemed so friendly.'

'Even so,' said the other adult, 'you can't be too careful around strange dogs.'

Lawrie and Jacob continued to play with the dog until the second adult told them it was time to leave.

'Oh, Mike,' said Jacob, 'he's lovely. Can we take him home with us?'

'Not today,' he replied.

Fin laughed aloud and began to cycle as fast as he could to catch up with the others.

CHAPTER 8- THE FAITHFUL HOUND
(Capel-Curig)

From his vantage point above the multiple waterfalls that made up the Swallow Falls, Fin watched the crowds of tourists return to their busses and vanish into the early evening. In a momentary gap in visitors, they had splashed through the water and hidden their bikes from prying eyes. Just in time, it seemed, for no sooner than they had crossed the water and hidden than Gabriel appeared following their trail. Saliva dripping from his mouth he sniffed at the water's edge, then followed the water downstream, stopping every now and then to look around. In silence, the friends hid in the undergrowth and waited for night to fall.

Slowly the weather worsened, a wind picked up, and it began to rain. His hands cold and wet Fin tried to rub them together to warm them up. It was futile, he considered using his powers but realised that would only reveal their hiding place to their pursuers.

'We can't stay here much longer,' said Gwyneth as she peered through the bushes, 'we are all getting too cold.'

No one argued.

'We need to get off the main road and disappear,' she continued, 'and I think I know just the place. But you are not going to like it.'

Not liking the sound of those words Jenny gave Gwyneth a hard look and waited.

'I suggest, we return to our bikes and cycle as far Tŷ Hyll,' she added, 'There we can leave them at the Ugly House and book a taxi.'

A disgruntled look crossed Sparrow's face, 'Last time we did that they knew exactly where we were going and when.'

'We don't have to go anywhere in the taxi,' she replied, 'but we can pay the driver to deliver a package to an old friend of mine. That should distract the hunt for long enough for us to go where they will not be able to follow us.'

With that Gwyneth jumped up, shook out her hair and turned into the younger version of herself, 'I think I'm going to need some of the vigour of my youth,' she said and paddled over to the bicycles, 'Come on, it's time we moved.'

~

The A5 road was quiet, but Gwyneth would not let them linger and soon breathless from the ride they stopped outside The Ugly House.

'You stay with the bikes,' said Gwyneth, 'I will be quick.'

Moments later she reappeared with a carrier bag

of food and showed them where their bicycles could be stored.

'I have arranged for a taxi to come for us, and the owner has agreed to pay the driver to deliver a parcel for me.'

'Didn't she think you were a bit strange?' asked Skye.

'She has always considered me a little strange,' she replied, 'but not as strange as the taxi driver thought I was.'

'You want me to pick five of you up now at the Ugly House?'

'Yes please.'

'You do realise that I am in Conwy?'

'Yes, I do,' she continued, 'and I am prepared to pay in advance.'

'Why me?'

'I am assured that you are totally reliable... and discreet.'

'I'll be with you in an hour.'

~

'Why,' grumbled Skye, 'did we have to get back into the river?'

'Because' explained Jenny for the fifth time, 'the hounds cannot follow our trail in the water.'

Uncomfortable and wet, the party kept to the edges of the river, but as careful as they were, they were all soon drenched. Cold and frustrated Fin stumbled, unable to maintain his balance he slipped once again under the water.

'Not far now,' said Gwyneth, 'we are near the Capel Curig Training Centre.'

Keeping the buildings in sight, they crawled

along the bank until they met a stream that led into a small wood. As silently as they could, they held to the water until they reached the A5 and then crossed the road.

Once across the road, Skye asked, 'Does that foul river have a name?'

'Afon Llugwy,' replied Gwyneth, 'and don't insult her, she has been a good friend to us. Without the river, we would never have reached here without being caught.'

'What now?' asked Fin, 'I trust that you have a good idea of how we can escape the hunt.'

'We climb just a little higher,' she replied, 'and then I hope to meet a few old friends.'

Keeping clear of the farm, they headed up the hill and just when Fin felt he could go no further, Gwyneth stopped and sniffed the air.

'This is the place,' she said.

'Where are we heading for?' asked Jenny.

'The Roman Fort at Bryn Gefeiliau,' she replied, 'I'm hoping the soldiers will look after us tonight.'

Slipping her hand into her jacket, Gwyneth produced her son's ring and put it on her finger, 'My son was never interested in the old tales, and so he thought this ring was just a family heirloom.' Holding her hand up, she pointed her finger at the sky. As the rain slowly fell the ring began to glow and lit up her face.

As Fin watched, the sky whirled into a flickering display of light and dark. Feeling slightly nauseous he focused his eyes on Gwyneth and watched her grow old before him. He had seen her change before, but this time was different, instead of the mischievous grin he had seen previously, he saw pain and anguish.

'Gwyneth?' he began, but she silenced him with a look.

'It is done,' said the elderly lady beside them, 'I have done all that I can.'

Concern filled Jenny's face as she watched Gwyneth fall to the floor. Rushing over she picked her up and was surprised at how little she weighed.

'It is okay my child,' whispered Gwyneth, 'I am old, but my powers will return. However, I think I will have to stay at the fort and rest for a few years.'

'Years?' exclaimed Jenny, 'Where are we?'

'I think you misunderstand,' she replied, 'it is rather more a question of when rather than where.'

Enlightenment filled Fin's face, 'Oh you faithful hound,' he laughed, 'to avoid the hunt you have taken us back in time.'

'Then that ring,' suggested Sparrow, 'controls time.'

'Nothing controls time,' she grimaced, 'but occasionally we can swing on its cloak tails.' A tired look crossed her face, 'Alas I am already old and spent, I fear I will be remaining here for a long time to come.

Here my dear, take this.' Stretching out her withered arm, Gwyneth dropped the ring into Jenny's hand. 'I declare you my heir and successor, take this ring which is yours and mine and use it wisely.'

Opening her hand, Jenny stared at the ring in her palm, and it began to glow.

'See it recognises you.'

'But how do I use it?'

'You will know when the time is right,' she replied cryptically, 'but using it will tire you and I fear it may cost you more than you are prepared to pay.'

Lost for words Jenny slipped the ring onto her finger and then gasped in amazement as it shrank in size to fit her finger.

'Use it sparingly,' warned Gwyneth as she slumped into Jenny's embrace.

'Halt, who goes there?' shouted an aggressive voice as eight soldiers carrying short swords burst into the clearing.

'Cephas,' whispered Gwyneth, 'I need you to escort these children to Beddgelert, for I fear I am now a burden to them.'

'My Lady,' he cried falling on his knees next to Jenny, 'as ever, your wish is my command.'

'Thank you,' she whispered, 'I am so grateful.'

Gently, Cephas took Gwyneth out of Jenny's arms, 'I my love, I will do anything for you.'

'My love?' asked Fin.

A smile crossed Cephas' face, 'My wife has lived many lives, had many faces but always returns here to rest from her perilous journeys. I never know when she will return to me, but she always does.' A concerned look crossed his face, 'But I have never seen her this old and tired. What year do you come from and who chases you?'

'Gabriel,' replied Jenny, 'and we are from the year twenty...'

'Gabriel,' exclaimed Cephas cutting Jenny's words off before she could finish, 'then we must hurry and get my lady to the fort, for I fear that Gabriel may even find you here.'

CHAPTER 9 - THE BREATH OF GABRIEL
(Beddgelert)

Quietly following Cephas and his friends, Fin gazed in wonder and the wild beauty of the hills. It seemed so peaceful, but he could not escape the feeling that they were being watched. Quickly catching Cephas up he mentioned his concerns.

'The locals don't really like us being here,' acknowledged Cephas as he struggled to support Gwyneth, 'and normally a small group like us moves too quickly to gain their attention.'

'I'm slowing you down,' said Gwyneth.

'It's not far to the fort,' he replied, 'we should be fine...'

An arrow crashed into a tree beside his head, and the soldiers dived for cover.

'Arrows are like ants,' he whispered, 'see one, and there are bound to be a lot more.'

'We are too exposed here,' said one of the soldiers.

'There are not enough of us to make a full shield wall,' he replied, 'but do it anyway.'

'Immediately, Decanus!'

'Surround the children first,' continued Cephas.

Arrows began to ping off the shields as the soldiers let them out of the inadequate shelter of the trees into an open space. Surprised by the tactic, Fin kept inside the shell of shields and watched as the soldiers drew out their swords.

Hearing Fin's unasked question Cephas explained, 'I would rather fight in the open where I have room to swing my sword. Their arrows are unlikely to harm us behind these shields, so I am hoping that there are only a few of them and that they will charge at us.'

'And if there is a lot of them?' Jenny asked joining in the conversation.

'Then we die.'

'Guerrilla warfare,' added Sparrow, 'pick off the stragglers and move on.'

'Marwolaeth i bawb!' cried a voice that was echoed by a crowd of excited voices.

'Death for all,' translated Skye, 'not a particularly cheerful thought.'

'I'm sorry,' said Cephas, 'it appears that we are seriously outnumbered. This is going to get very messy.'

Peeking out through the shields, Fin watched about fifty, small dark-haired men appear out of the landscape.

'There's too many of them,' continued Cephas.

'Then I will deal with them,' said Fin. 'Give me some space.'

'You are a boy,' he replied, 'what can you do?'

'Give him space,' commanded Gwyneth in a tired but determined voice.

'As you wish my lady.'

Expanding the shield wall the soldiers gave Fin the space he requested. As he burst into flames and rose up into the air a look of terror filled the soldiers' faces. Higher into the air Fin rose, and as he did so, he began to glow so brightly that nobody could look directly at him.

'There will be no fighting today,' said Fin, 'there will be no blood spilt on this land.' Then he laughed and cried out, 'Death can have a day off!'

Beneath him, the soldiers' fear turned to wonder as the Welsh fighters disappeared back into the countryside.

Once Fin was convinced that the threat was over, he gently dropped to the ground and collapsed into unconsciousness.

~

Fin awoke in an open space, his head was lying on Jenny's lap, and around him, five hundred soldiers were attending the business of the fort.

'So, the Phoenix awakes,' said a voice behind him.

Lifting his head Fin turned to see Cephas sipping water out of a pottery cup.

'That was an amazing trick you pulled off back there,' he continued.

'It's just as well the Welsh fighters didn't know I used up all my energy on a firework display,' muttered Fin as his head fell back into Jenny's lap.

'Nevertheless, it saved the day, and nobody

died.'

The words, though accurate, went unheard as Fin slipped back into an exhausted sleep. Fin lost track of how many days they stayed in the Roman Fort, and for a moment the fear of the chase left him. The others, he recalled later, laughed a lot and he enjoyed watching them relax in the summer sunshine. Gwyneth was his only concern, and while she seemed older than he had ever known her, she too seemed to be slowly improving.

~

Overhead thunder clouds growled in anger and lightning lit up the darkened hillside, and the chase felt a lifetime away. Heavy rain began to fall, and soon they were all soaked to the skin.

'We are being followed,' whispered Cephas as he signalled them to stop.

Squinting into the darkness Fin could see nothing and the rain hid any sound of their watcher.

'I can smell your fear,' growled a voice.

A flash of lightning illuminated the hillside revealing a giant hound.

'Gabriel,' groaned Fin.

'You know me,' replied Gabriel, 'whereas I do not know you.'

Out of the darkness, the Hounds of Gabriel gathered around them, steam rising from their coats.

'How do you know me?'

'We have met before,' said Fin.

'Then why do I not remember?' said Gabriel. 'That interests me.' Padding around the party

Gabriel considered them, 'Eight soldiers with whom I have no quarrel. A boy and three girls...' Sniffing the air he snorted, 'Though I sense... great power but little maturity.'

'If you are going to insult us...'

'I mean no insult, I merely observe.'

The pack drew closer to the party and Gabriel sniffed Fin's clothes.

'Well it has been lovely to meet you,' interrupted Jenny, 'but we need to be going.'

'Hmmm, brave you are,' said Gabriel, 'the soldiers may go, the children will stay with me.'

'Not a chance,' snapped Cephas drawing his sword, 'where they go we go.'

'It's okay,' said Sparrow reassuringly, 'we had to leave you somewhere, and I promise you we will be fine. Please give our love to Gwyneth and tell her we will pray for her recovery.'

Cephas searched Fin's face for confirmation.

'We will be fine,' he said, 'you honour us with your loyalty, and you know we can handle ourselves.'

A smile of understanding crossed the face of Cephas, 'As you wish. Will we meet again?'

'I doubt it, but we will always remember you.'

Nodding his head, Cephas returned his sword to its sheath and took a last look at Gabriel. At his signal, the eight soldiers vanished into the night, and they saw them no more.

The hounds of Gabriel gathered around Fin, Jenny, Sparrow and Skye and began to circle them.

'Thank you for letting the soldiers go,' said Jenny, 'but now I think it is time we left you too.'

'I think not,' replied Gabriel, 'How do you know me, I wonder?'

'We have seen you from afar,' said Fin truthfully.

Gabriel paced curiously around Fin.

'You interest me,' he said, 'all of you do. I know you yet have received no command to chase you.'

'Then you have no grounds for delaying us,' said Jenny, 'and we really do need to be somewhere else.'

'Quiet child,' snapped Gabriel, 'for I am thinking.'

Sensing Jenny's anger, Fin placed his hand on her arm, and she relaxed.

Aware of the interchange, Gabriel sensed Jenny's immense power dissipate.

'My words offended you,' he continued, 'and you are used to being listened to. My error, I apologise, you are obviously not from around here.'

'Indeed,' replied Jenny.

You are from... you are from my future.'

Behind Fin, Skye took a deep breath.

'Oh, I see that I am correct,' reasoned Gabriel.

One of the hounds approached their gathering, 'My Lord, the outrunners tell me that a band of Celts approach us.'

'Then it is time we moved on,' replied Gabriel, 'bring the children with us.'

'Yes my Lord.'

The hounds growled and disappeared into the night, leaving only one to guard their master. A cry echoed around the hill, an arrow flew through the air and struck Gabriel in the neck. Blood squirted from the wound and Gabriel fell dying to the earth.

'No!' cried Fin dropping to his knees. Snapping the head off the arrow that pierced Gabriel's neck, he removed the shaft and healed the wound.

Painfully Gabriel rose to his feet, 'You saved me, why?'

'You are not my enemy,' replied Fin still struggling with the aftershock of the pain.

'Nevertheless,' continued Gabriel, 'you are still coming with me until I find out who you are.'

'I'm sorry but we can't,' said Jenny as she gripped the ring on her finger, 'We need to be somewhere else.'

Clutching the others to her, Jenny's hand began to glow with a bright blue light and the damp evening was replaced with a field filled with snow.

CHAPTER 10 - GELERT'S CAVE
(Gelert)

'Where are we?' Fin asked as he dithered in the cold.

'We are still just above Beddgelert,' replied Jenny, 'and I'm going to be sick.' Pushing Skye to one side, Jenny deposited the contents of her stomach on to the snow.

'I can't see the town,' said Sparrow squinting into the brightness of the landscape.

'I don't think it's been built yet,' said Jenny, 'I got us away from Gabriel, but I have no idea what year it is.'

Pulling her glasses down over her eyes, Skye unexpectedly took charge of the situation. 'Jenny is exhausted, Fin is powerless to help us after saving Gabriel and Sparrow, and I do not have superpowers.' She grabbed Jenny's coat and zipped it up. 'We need to find shelter, and we need to find it now.'

Dragging Jenny into her arms, Skye walked towards a rocky outcrop and told the others to follow. The snow was deeper than any of them had expected, and for Fin and Jenny, it was torture.

Falling to the ground Fin muttered, 'I can't go on.'

'You must,' cried Skye as she tried and failed to pick him up, 'if you don't you will die of hypothermia.'

Reluctantly, Fin forced himself to stand. 'Where are we going?'

'Cephas told me that there was a cave in this outcrop,' she replied.

'But that was years ago,' complained Fin, 'we might not be in the same place.'

'Idiot,' snapped Skye, 'we moved in time, not in place. That is the same hill we walked down earlier.'

By sheer force of will, Skye bullied Fin and Jenny into moving. Looking to Sparrow for support, Skye was frustrated to see that she was distracted and appeared to be talking to herself.

'Can't you do anything?' demanded Sparrow, 'I know you can hear me!'

'There's nobody there,' reasoned Skye.

'Of course, there is!'

'We are on our own.'

'No we are not, I can see him.'

'Who can you see?'

'My friend, Reese.'

Skye tried to see what Sparrow could see, but the hillside was empty.

'Please Sparrow,' said Skye, 'there is nobody there, and I need your help to get these two to some sort of shelter.'

Ignoring Skye's plea, Sparrow shouted into the wind, 'We will die if you don't help us.'

'Nobody's dying today,' said a hooded figure appearing out of the snow.

'Thank you,' said Sparrow to the empty hillside.

'My pleasure,' replied the figure.

'I wasn't talking to you.'

'I know,' the figure replied, 'I wasn't talking to you either!'

~

The fire crackled in the entranceway to the cave, and although smoky, the cave was warm.

'My name is Gelert,' continued the voice, 'I am a Christian missionary from Llandysul, and I came here to share the good news with the local Celts. Not that they thought what I was bringing was good news. I have done all I can here, and I was due to be heading home when the snow came and delayed me.'

'Who were you talking to on the hillside?' asked Skye.

'A question you have no doubt asked your friend too,' Gelert supposed, 'What did she say?'

'She thought she saw her boyfriend, Reese Edwards,' she replied, 'but now she thinks she saw things.'

'Does she now?' replied Gelert, 'I too saw an old friend, but I am a hermit and am often used to seeing people and talking to myself!'

~

Fin woke to the warmth of the wood fire. Outside the cave, the snow continued to fall, and all trace of their exertions were obliterated. The darkness of night dropped, and the light in the cave became muted.

'I was wondering when you would wake,' said Gelert, 'here drink this.'

Taking the pottery cup in hands Fin sipped the soup. 'Thank you,' he said, 'you saved us just in time.'

'My pleasure.'

'Then you are Gelert?'

'Excellent.'

'You speak as if you have heard of me.'

'I have,' replied Fin, 'the town below will take its name from you.'

'Indeed,' replied Gelert, 'it seems to me that they want to kill me.'

'Nevertheless, they named the town Beddgelert after you.'

A smile crossed Gelert's face, 'Then are you telling me that I am to be martyred here?'

'I'm sorry I don't understand,' replied Fin, 'Why would you think that?'

'Beddgelert, literally means, "Gelert's Grave!"'

'Oh,' continued Fin, 'I'm sorry I didn't know.'

~

Daylight poured into the cave and Fin and Jenny, now energised gathered their things together. Outside the snow had stopped and the sounds of life had returned to the countryside. Dogs barked, and the birds sang in the trees.

'Oh no,' cried Gelert, 'we are in trouble.'

'By the locals?' asked Fin.

'Worse,' cried Gelert throwing logs onto the fire, 'wolves!'

'Wolves?'

'Gather your things together,' cried Gelert, 'and

run.'

Moments later they were falling down the hill trying to keep up with the hermit.

'This has happened before,' he shouted back over his shoulder, 'we will be safe from the wolves in the village. They are too scared to attack the villagers.'

'I thought they hated you there and wanted to kill you!' replied Skye.

'They do,' he continued, 'but you can argue the point with a human, whereas a wolf just has bad breath and big teeth.'

'Good point,' said Skye.

'That said,' he muttered, 'some of the locals also have bad breath...'

~

Bursting into the village, they ran down the main street with the wolves following and howling behind them. Villagers grabbed pitchforks and staffs and poured out into the street. The women picked up wooden buckets and struck them with sticks and the men brandished their homemade weapons. Growling, the leader ignored the noise, approached the villagers and only retreated when an arrow landed in the snow next to him.

The wolves departed, and the villagers surrounded Gelert and ignored the children.

'Here you poor things,' said a young woman to them, 'come with me and warm up by my fire.'

'What about Gelert?' asked Sparrow.

'The menfolk have had enough of him and his teachings,' she replied, 'they blame him for the bad weather.'

'That's ridiculous,' said Sparrow.

'That's men for you,' she said, 'but don't you think that you can help him now. He's safe enough for the moment.'

Reluctantly they left Gelert a prisoner of the villagers and entered one of the cottages.

~

Sitting by the fire, Fin felt guilty and could not help wondering what was happening to Gelert. Anwyn, their new friend, had disappeared to discover what was happening to him and had been gone a while. As evening fell the others had fallen asleep, and the room was full of the sound of snoring and sighing. The door creaked open, and Anwyn reappeared.

'Not good news I'm afraid,' she said, 'They are going to tie him up and leave him for the wolves.'

'Then I must help him,' replied Fin.

'I'm not so sure why children are so keen to defend a hermit,' she paused, 'Look the old folk of the village aren't interested in you. At least not while they are fixated on Gelert, and you need to keep it that way.'

'Why are you helping us?' asked Sparrow.

'I liked Gelert,' she replied, 'But right now I'm worried about you too. Where are you heading for?'

'Plucking a name out of his mind,' Fin replied, 'Penrhyndeudreath.'

'That's a day's travel at the best of times,' said Anwyn, 'I think it would be best for you if when they are throwing Gelert to the wolves that you disappear at the same time. The diversion will help you escape both the villagers and the wolves.'

~

Through the open doorway, they watched the villagers carry the tied and struggling Gelert out into the street. Dumping his body there, they left him and returned to their homes to wait. Within moments the wolves appeared and circled Gelert.

'We have to rescue him,' said Jenny.

'I agree,' replied Fin, 'I will do it.'

'No,' said Jenny stopping Fin from leaving the building, 'I will.'

'Are you sure?'

'Yes,' she replied, 'I'll be quieter and less dramatic.'

Slipping out the door, Jenny ran across the street and threw herself over Gelert.

'What is she doing?' asked Anwyn, 'She'll be killed too.'

The wind whipped up, and snow obscured the view. The hounds howled, and they sounded angry and vicious. The wind dropped and there crying over the body of Gelert was Jenny, distressed but unharmed.

Anwyn and Fin led the others out, and Skye consoled a distraught Jenny. The night grew cold and only returning for shovels, they dealt with Gelert's body. Working quickly, they buried the body as deep as they could and built a mound on top of it.

'That was so kind of you,' said Anwyn when they had finished, 'and so cruel of the villagers. I will make sure that they never forget Gelert and his message of peace and hope.'

CHAPTER 11 - PORTMEIRION
(Penrhyndeudreath)

Travelling through the night, they worked their way towards Penrhyndeudreath.

'Are you going to tell me what really happened?' asked Fin.

Satisfied that they were not being followed by the villagers or the wolves, Fin indicated that they should stop for a moment.

'That was a lovely show you put on there for Anwyn,' he continued, 'though I'm not sure why.'

'Plausible deniability,' responded Jenny, 'Anwyn had to believe it to be true.'

'Believe what to be true?' asked Skye.

'That Gelert is dead,' she replied, 'but of course, he is not.'

'Then whose body did we bury?'

'A large wolf that I had turned to stone.'

'Then where is Gelert?' continued a puzzled Skye.

'I sent him off into the night,' she replied, 'he can't half run for a hermit!'

An approaching lone wolf, hearing the unrestrained laughter, decided to forage somewhere else for its food.

'I think it's time,' said Jenny rummaging through her pockets.

'Time for what?' asked Fin.

'Time to make another attempt to get home.'

'Where or when?'

'Oh definitely when,' continued Jenny, 'my new abilities seem to leave us where we are. But we need to get back to our own time period.' Producing the ring from her pocket, she slipped it on her finger.

'But you are still weak from the last jump.'

'That's why I need your help.'

Understanding what she was asking him, Fin nodded his head and drew the others into an embrace. 'This is going to hurt,' he said warning them, 'but no matter what happens you must not break my contact with Jenny.'

The snow-filled landscape whirled around them and transformed into a swirling pattern of light and dark. It was impossible not to feel sick, and Skye spewed vomit into the time-stream.

'Sorry,' she yelled, but no one was listening.

Jenny began to scream. First, blood leaked from her nose and dripped across her lip, but soon Fin joined her. Doubling over in agony, Fin began to glow, and wings of fire spread out from his back. Still, they travelled in a world of light and dark, yet somehow they were moving more slowly. Jenny's screaming became louder, and Fin struggled to hold her to him. The others struggled to hold on to each other as Fin's body began to get increasingly hotter and he too screamed in agony.

'Enough!' cried Sparrow as she burnt her hands breaking Fin's grip on Jenny.

The time eddies stopped, and they crashed to the ground.

~

Opening her eyes, Skye was the first to recover. Pulling herself up on a fencepost she stared at the steps that fell away from her and down into a fantasy village. In the distance, she could see a film crew and actors dressed in striped blazers and boater hats. A groan from behind a flower bed alerted her to find the others. The moan had come from Sparrow who was trying to sit up without using her hands. Carefully, Skye pulled Sparrow to her feet and inspected her burnt and blistered hands.

'You broke the connection,' said Skye.

Unable to speak through the pain, Sparrow simple nodded.

To the left of them, in a clump of trees, a smouldering bonfire filled the air with smoke.

'We need to find Fin and Jenny,' continued Skye, 'you sit on these steps until I get back.'

Unable to argue, Sparrow sat down and began to cry. Torn between searching for the others and caring for Sparrow, Skye paused.

'Find them,' said Sparrow through gritted teeth. 'But please be quick.'

Sparrow watched as Skye searched behind bushes and trees, flower-beds and fences. It was only when the pain became too much that she closed her eyes and prayed. 'Oh God, please we need a miracle...' she whispered,

'Found them,' cried Skye.

Opening her eyes, Sparrow watched Skye pull Fin out of the bonfire. Once on his feet, Fin pulled Jenny up to join him.

Moments later, Fin knelt down over Sparrow and took her hands in his and healed them.

'Thank you,' whispered Sparrow.

~

'My mistake,' began Fin, 'I told you not to separate us, but I did not take into consideration that I might burn you. Sparrow, I'm so sorry that I hurt you and put you through so much pain.'

Looking at her newly healed hands, Sparrow replied, 'In healing me you felt everything I felt. I forgive you because I know you need to hear me say it. But what else could we do, we had to try to get home?'

'I'm sorry to interrupt such a meaningful moment,' said Jenny, 'but I think I know where and when we are.'

'Portmeirion, 1967 on the set of "The Prisoner,"' cried Skye, stealing her thunder. 'I've just seen Patrick McGoohan wearing a number 6 badge.'

'How do you know about a television series from the 1960's?' asked Jenny.

'I had an uncle who was a mad fan of the show,' she replied, 'and I've watched every episode.'

'I've never heard of it,' said Fin, 'what's it about?'

'It's a bit "off the wall" really,' she continued,

'but it was a spy drama that used Portmeirion as a prison and Number 6 spent his whole time trying to escape from it.'

'I think we are going to need some new clothes,' said Jenny changing the subject, 'we look a mess.'

'Well there you are!' cried a harried-looking lady with a clipboard in her hand, 'If you want to get paid, it's no good sneaking off for a quick break.' She considered their dishevelled state and continued, 'You have ten minutes to nip down to the wardrobe waggon and get your blazers and boaters.' Pausing she smiled, 'I thought you did really well in the fire scene, it will look amazing when its broadcast. Now off you pop.'

Confused and not wishing to draw even more attention to themselves they ran down the steps to the wardrobe van and gathered some clean clothes. Once dressed they were chased down to the beach by Sally, the lady with the clipboard, and told to report to the stunt director.

'What's going on?' asked Jenny.

'They must have confused us with some of their stunt artists,' replied Skye, 'I understand that they used a lot of guest actors and even some of the locals from the village.'

~

Feeling slightly foolish they stood on the beach and watched the support crew drag a giant balloon towards them.

'What's all this about?' asked Fin.

'That balloon is supposed to chase escapees and capture them,' replied Skye.

'Then I guess we are about to be chased,' he

continued.

'Yeah,' she added, 'it always looked good on the television, but it was always a bit "cheesy!"'

A crazed howl filled the air and everyone, crew and actors, looked up into the trees. Silhouetted against the sky stood a gigantic hound, Gabriel had found them.

'How has he found us?' asked Sparrow, 'We are still not back in our own time!'

'He must have a good memory,' replied Fin, 'but we need to get away.'

Realising that everyone was distracted, Fin led the others in a run across the beach to the trees and the safety of the hills.

From his vantage point, Gabriel watched the children run and blew into the air. The giant balloon leapt out of the hands of the crew and flew after them down the beach. The film crew seeing the pursuit, rolled the film in their cameras and watched as Fin and the others attempted to dodge the savage balloon.

Repeatedly, the balloon knocked the children to the ground and circled them as they attempted to escape its persistence.

'I've just about had enough of this,' cried Sparrow as she picked up a broken bottle from the beach and slashed at the balloon. The balloon burst, with an exaggerated explosion of air, and blasted them into the woods at the edge of the beach.

CHAPTER 12 - THE IRON MAN
(Llanbedrog)

The wind whipped the rain through the trees and Fin's hiding place became a muddy puddle. Overhead the clouds blended into the dark of the night and Fin could not see his hands in front of his face.

'We have been here for hours,' he complained, 'if Gabriel were going to have found us he would have done so by now.'

Disgruntled silence hung in the air around him.

'It was your idea to hide here!' said Skye from the cocoon of leaves she had created around her. 'You made us walk up a stream, climb up a waterfall and hide in these trees.'

'Well it worked,' he replied, 'Gabriel hasn't found us.'

'Maybe, maybe not,' she continued, 'but I've only just got warm, and I'm not budging from this position just to get cold and wet again!'

Thunder crashed around them, the trees flashed into stark visibility and then vanished again. Rain poured through the leafy branches, and soon even

Skye began to get soaked. The ground around them turned into a stream and as they moved it transformed quickly into a muddy quagmire. Reluctantly, they fought their way out of the mud on to dryer ground and began to trudge their way west.

'It's no good,' grumbled Skye, 'we can't keep heading west.'

'Why not?' snapped Fin.

'Because, we will hit the silted up bay,' she replied.

'We need some shelter for the night,' interjected Jenny, 'We are all too cold and wet to continue, I suggest we head inland and see what we can find.'

Unable to argue with her logic Fin agreed and they headed north. Leaving the shelter of the trees behind them they briskly walked up a quiet road.

'Careful,' said Fin, 'I can see bright lights ahead.'

Quietly, they crept up the road and looked into the grounds of an old castle. Bright lights illuminated a film set, and the crew they had met earlier in the day were turning the castle into a hospital.

'We've been so worried about you,' said a voice from behind them, 'how fantastic you were able to find your way back here to Castell Deudraeth.'

Startled they were greeted by Sally whom they had met earlier, still with a clipboard in her hand.

'We lost you in the storm,' she continued. Ticking a box on her clipboard, she considered their appearance, shook her head and pointed towards the castle. 'Go and get cleaned up and I'll meet you in the kitchen trailer and get you some food.'

Herding Fin and his friends up the path they were warmly greeted by the support crew and given clean clothes.

'The storm came out of nowhere,' said the wardrobe manager, 'and Sally was devastated that you went missing. She wanted to call the police but the second film unit's director wouldn't let her. Anyway, go and get something to eat and we'll see what the filming itinerary is for tomorrow.'

Finding it impossible to slip away, they joined Sally and her clipboard at the kitchen trailer, and they sat down and ate a large meal.

'They've abandoned filming anything else on the beach for this episode,' said Sally, 'but they got some great footage of you running away from the balloon. The director could not believe how the special effects unit had managed to get it to chase you so realistically.'

'It was too realistic for me,' muttered Jenny.

'Yes, well... it was quite spectacular,' continued Sally, 'Anyway with the wrapping up of the filming early you are all finished here, and tomorrow, you can take the train from Minffordd to Llanbedrog.'

'Llanbedrog?' asked Fin.

'I thought you knew.'

'Sorry,' replied Fin, 'I think the tiredness is making me a little forgetful.'

'They want you to be ready to begin filming at the Tin Man by eight-thirty,' she smiled, 'but don't worry, I'll make sure the car gets you to the station on time.'

Bewildered, they allowed themselves to be led to

some rooms reserved for the crew inside the castle and took advantage of the bathing facilities provided.

~

Standing in Llanbedrog, Fin gazed up at the Tin Man and admired its craftsmanship.

'Why on earth has this been put here?' asked Sparrow.

'I've no idea why anyone would put a Tin Man here,' replied Fin.

'Iron Man,' declared Skye.

'Whatever,' snapped Jenny, 'Who cares?'

Fin considered the statue and wondered. It was apparently a figurehead from an old ship and featured a bearded man staring up at the sky.

'Whatever reason it's here,' he said, 'it has seen better days.'

'Whoever put it here, did so for a purpose,' said Sparrow, 'but why you would prop it up here, I have no idea.'

A chill wind blew across the hilltop and clouds blocked the sun.

'I thought I would find you here,' said Gabriel as he padded his way towards them. 'For centuries I have followed your trail. You are not my quarry, and yet our paths are interconnected.' Sniffing the air Gabriel sighed. 'You have angered someone,' he said, 'I watched you escape that stage prop and then disappear.'

'I thought that was you,' said Fin.

'No,' he replied, 'I am not hunting you.'

'But...'

'If I were chasing you, you would know.'

Unable to hold Gabriel's gaze, Fin looked away.

'However, it appears that you believe I am chasing you.'

'The Wild Hunt is on our trail,' replied Fin in a moment of surprising honesty.

'I very much doubt that as I would know,' exclaimed Gabriel, 'for I am the leader of the hunt.'

'I'm not sure why I am telling you this,' added Fin, 'but in your future, you will be chasing us.'

'But not today,' replied Gabriel, 'your honesty does you proud.' Stretching his neck, he continued, 'It was you that removed an arrow from my neck.'

Saying nothing Fin just nodded.

'I thought so.'

'Why?'

'It was the right thing to do.'

A stench of rotten fish filled the air, and a giant shadow enveloped them. Twisting around in fear, Fin stumbled backwards as an enormous white dragon hovered above them. Its eyes glinted with menace and steam erupted from its nostrils.

'Gwiber, what an unpleasant surprise,' growled Gabriel, his hackles rising up on his powerful neck. 'Why are you here?'

'For you, my furry little friend,' replied the dragon, 'you are far from home and separated from your pack.'

'What of it?'

'At worst I'm going to singe your fur, and at best, I am going to burn you alive.'

'Oh for goodness sake,' interrupted Fin, 'I'm tired, and I just want to go home, and you are beginning to irritate me.'

'Stay out of this little man,' snapped Gwiber, fire dripping from his mouth, 'and leave this conversation to your elders and betters.'

'I admit that you are older than me,' replied Fin, 'but no dragon is my better.'

'You will not live to regret saying that,' snarled Gwiber.

'Leave these young people out of this,' said Gabriel, 'this discussion is between you and me.'

'Indeed it is,' replied Gwiber, pouring fire out of his mouth as he tried to burn them all.

Fire rained down on the party and obscured his victims from his view. When the fire cleared, they all stood unharmed, and Fin held his arms up in the air. 'My name is Fenix Butler, I am the Phoenix, the son of the Phoenix and my mother was a dragon. Your fire cannot harm me, nor can your lies or venom touch my friends and me. Go home while you are still alive and leave us alone.'

'Never,' cried Gwiber and poured fire down again.

Inside the protective bubble Jenny laughed at Fin, 'I told you one day that wouldn't work.'

'I am the Phoenix...'

'Oh do shut up,' said Jenny. Gathering everyone around Fin and Gabriel, Jenny played with her ring and admitted, 'You are tired, and your powers are weak. On a good day, you can destroy any dragon but not today.'

'Agreed,' he replied, 'but are you up to a time jump?'

'Not really but we must try.'

Jenny held up her hand and concentrated on her

ring, but nothing happened. With one hand Fin continued to hold his protective field around them, with the other he pulled Jenny towards him and kissed her. Instantly, the world swirled into a mixture of fire and darkness, and that suddenly fell silent.

'When are we?' asked Skye.

'I've no idea,' replied Jenny, 'but whenever we are, we need to get out of here fast. The dragon's fire has destroyed the Iron Man, and I'm sure the locals are not going to be too happy to see their statue so badly vandalised.'

CHAPTER 13 – ST MARY'S WELL
(Aberdaron)

'Where's Gabriel?' asked Fin spinning around on the spot.

'He's vanished,' replied Jenny. 'I don't remember seeing him after we materialised.'

Angry voices echoed over the headland.

'Move,' said Sparrow taking command, 'we will have too much explaining to do if we stay here.'

Slipping into the shadows of the night they disappeared into the darkness. Just in time, as a group of local villagers brandishing torches ran towards the remains of the Iron Man.

'Why would anyone vandalise the Iron Man?' cried an angry voice.

'Bloody tourists...'

Quietly, Fin and his friends escaped their voices and their recriminations.

~

'No matter what we do,' said Sparrow, 'we keep following the trail.' Slipping her hand into her jacket, she pulled out her parchment with the annotations on the side and started to read. 'Llyn Tegid, Blaenau Ffestiniog, Betws-y-Coed, Capel-

Curig, Beddgelert, Penrhyndeudreath, Llanbedrog, Aberdaron, Ynys Enlli, Llangwnadl, Llanaelhaiarn and Carnarvon.'

'Yes, yes,' replied Fin grumpily, 'the mystic's trail.'

'But don't you see,' continued Sparrow, 'we have followed them all, and our next stop is going to be Aberdaron.'

'So you are suggesting that we deliberately follow the trail,' said Fin.

'Why not? We seem to be following it whether we like it or not. Let's be proactive and choose to follow it.'

Rustling in his bag, Fin produced a map he had acquired in Portmeirion and laid it out. 'It's about eleven miles from here to there, and it's a pretty rough trail.' He rubbed his chin, 'I reckon we can walk it in about four hours.'

'I'm hungry,' muttered Skye.

'I need a toilet,' added Sparrow.

Pulling a chocolate bar out of his pocket, Fin passed the bar to Skye, 'That's you sorted.' Pointing at a group of trees, he laughed and said, 'And that's you!'

'Paper would be nice,' muttered Sparrow as she disappeared into the woods.

~

Five hours later they arrived at the Llyn Peninsula, Aberdaron and walked along the long beach eating sandwiches they had purchased from a corner shop. Stopping at a small inlet, they considered the sharp rocks that guarded the way to St Mary's Well. The local shopkeeper had told them to avoid it. That was all Skye needed to encourage her to want to take a look. Ignoring the sea caves and rock pools they climbed the rocks until just above the high tide mark they found the well.

'Amazing,' exclaimed Fin as he tasted the water, 'it looks like every other rock pool, but it is drinkable.'

'I'm not drinking it,' said Jenny, 'it looks "iffy!"'

'And that,' said Sparrow, pointing out to sea, 'is Bardsey Island, Ynys Enlli the next stop on our map.'

'How do we get there?' asked Skye.

'No idea,' replied Fin, 'it's over a mile away, and that sea looks pretty rough.'

~

Sitting beside the well, they finished their sandwiches and gazed out to the island. Sipping the last of his drink Fin had a distinct impression that he was being watched. Suddenly, a dark cloud overshadowed them, and fire bounced off the rocks all around them. Immediately, Fin threw a barrier around his friends and turned to see who had attacked them. Outside Fin's protective bubble hovered a laughing Gwiber.

'What do you want?' asked Fin.

'Answers,' replied Gwiber, 'I have pondered on you for many years, and you confuse me.'

'Then what seems to be bothering you so much that you had to destroy our picnic?' said Fin. However, behind his back, he signalled the others to get ready to run.

'You claimed to be the Phoenix,' said Gwiber, 'but I know the Phoenix and he is old and feeble and currently has no wife or children. Therefore, you are an impostor, and yet you can control fire as he does.'

'I am what I am,' replied Fin, 'and your lack of understanding is your problem, not mine.'

'My lord is missing...'

'Again that is your problem.'

'And you are being chased by the Wild Hunt,' continued Gwiber, 'but then again maybe not.'

'What is it that you want?' asked Fin, 'For I am growing bored of your ramblings.'

Beside Fin, Jenny poked him in the ribs and whispered, 'Are you trying to annoy him?'

'Yes I am,' he replied, 'when I annoy him enough to breathe fire again, pull the others behind that rock and I will distract him.'

Understanding what he was intending, Jenny nodded and whispered, 'We will head for the last sea cave we saw and wait for you there.'

'My Lord, the Wyvern is missing,' continued Gwiber, 'and the Phoenix knows where he is hidden.'

Unable to keep his face from reflecting his emotions, Fin grimaced at the name of the Wyvern.

'So you do know something!' exclaimed the dragon, 'Then you will not leave here without sharing that information with me.'

A smile crossed Fin's face, and he signalled Jenny to get ready, 'Oh yes,' he replied, 'I have met your so-called Lord Wyvern, and have beaten him on every occasion. A pathetic sea-maggot he was, full of bitterness and past glory. However, that's all I'm prepared to say about him. So do your worst for I am not afraid of you.'

Fire filled the spaces around them and St Mary's Well bubbled and steamed in the heat of it. Expanding the protective bubble, Fin watched Jenny lead Sparrow and Skye away. Alone, Fin attempted to force the dragon's fire back at Gwiber and failed. It was all he could do to keep the flames from engulfing him. Feeling consciousness begin to slip away from him he staggered into the water of the well. The rock pool burst into steam, and he slipped under the water. Swallowing water, he surfaced, coughing and powerless he faced the dragon.

'What year is this?' asked the gloating dragon.

'I've no idea,' spluttered Fin.

'I thought so,' replied Gwiber, 'Would it surprise you to know you are in the 1980s?'

'Not at all,' said Fin.

'You smell of the future,' he continued, 'You will tell me everything I need to know. Refuse, and you will suffer in unimaginable pain. Speak, and you die quickly and as painlessly as I can make it.'

'I will never tell you anything.'

'Then I am going to hurt you,' continued Gwiber, 'and I believe that I am going to enjoy this.'

Again fire engulfed Fin and he screamed in agony as the water he was immersed in grow hotter. Laughing at Fin's pain Gwiber failed to notice that Jenny had reappeared and that her eyes had turned black. Angry at Gwiber's treatment of Fin she tried to convert him to stone. However, Gwiber was fortunate, for Jenny too, was tired and weary and her efforts to turn him to stone failed.

Falling backwards off the rock he had been balancing on, Gwiber fell to the rocks below. Confused he tried to fly but his wings felt strangely heavy, and he toppled down into the rising tide.

Grabbing Fin, Jenny led her soaking and hurting friend to the others at the entrance of one of the deeper sea caves. Unable to continue, Fin allowed himself to be dragged down into the cave and out of the light. Fire poured into the cave, as Gwiber, refreshed by the sea water, attacked them again.

'Deeper,' said Jenny, ' we need to get away from the entrance and find somewhere to hide.'

However, escape seemed impossible, as Jenny watched Gwiber crawl into the cave and begin to follow them down into the darkness.

CHAPTER 14 - THE SEA CAVE
(Bardsey Island)

Pulling her glasses down over her face, Skye pushed her way past the others and stood in the path of Gwiber.

'What are you doing?' demanded Jenny.

'So far on this trip, I have been a tourist and have tried to stay out of the way as you have used your powers to save us,' she replied, 'But this is my time, my opportunity to do something.'

Positioning herself between Gwiber and the others, Skye fixed her eyes on the dragon that was creeping towards them in the darkness. 'I sense that this cave is special,' Skye continued, 'I will buy us some time while you search for an exit.'

~

Unable to argue, Jenny and Sparrow carried Fin further into the cave.

'I know you are tired,' said Jenny, 'but can you give us any light?'

Unable to speak, Fin flipped a fire globe into the air in front of them, and it illuminated the cave. Ahead of them, the cave split into three. Checking each passage, Jenny indicated that they should take the left-hand one that led up. Fin struggled on as if in a dream, Gwiber's thoughts seemed to be attacking his will to resist, but still, he walked on. After climbing for an age, the cave ended in a dead end, and they flopped, dispirited to the floor.

'What's that?' asked Sparrow pointing at a carving in the wall.

Leaving Fin propped up against the wall, Jenny investigated.

'It looks familiar,' she said, 'I've seen this image of a flower somewhere before.' Rubbing the engraving with her fingers, Jenny cleaned and examined it. 'It is very similar to the marks on the walls next to the secret passages at Ravenswood House.' Slipping her fingers into the indentations, Jenny searched for the release catch. Finding none, she sat down next to Fin who was trying to hear what was happening to Skye.

~

'Why do you stand in my way little girl?' asked the Gwiber.

'To protect my friends from you,' replied Skye.

'And how the hell do you intend to do that?'

'With this,' said Skye holding up Glyndwr's dagger.

'No blade can hurt me.'

'This one can.'

'Foolish girl, even if you could strike me hard enough to hurt me, the blade would shatter!'

'Glyndwr's dagger will not shatter.'

A moment of doubt crossed Gwiber's mind as he sought to remember the blade. 'I have heard of Glyndwr's dagger,' he said, 'and it can only harm me if it is wielded by the Nimuë, the Lady of the Lake.'

'I thought you were clever,' replied Skye, 'and could sense when you were in danger.'

'I am in no danger from you!'

'My name is Skye Cairn,' she replied, 'and as you have guessed already, I am frightened of you. But what you don't know is that I am a descendant of Morgan Le Fay, or as you call her the Nimuë, the Lady of the Lake.'

'Nonsense,' snorted Gwiber.

'And if you know your history, Morgan Le Fay tricked Merlin into falling in love with her. Once he was smitten by her charms, he granted her, and her descendant's many powers. The most obvious is the ability to wake King Arthur from his sleep for I am the Nimuë stone.'

'You expect me to believe you?' laughed Gwiber, 'For I sense that you are the type to lie when you are scared.'

'To my shame,' she replied, 'I don't have to be scared to lie or exaggerate.' A tear slid down her face, 'I have often lied and hurt people by not telling the truth.' Wiping the tear from her eye, Skye shrugged, 'But for the first time in years, I am telling you the absolute truth.'

'Why should I believe you?'

'Because I have made friends who believe in me,' she replied, 'and for their sake, I am standing here.'

Gwiber laughed, and anger flared behind Skye's eyes.

'Then test me in this?' she cried, 'for though small, I am strong and you cannot hurt me.'

The dragon leapt at Skye and bounced off an invisible barrier. Falling to the ground, he lashed out with a clawed paw. Swinging Glyndwr's dagger, Skye sliced Gwiber's leg from his body and watched it fly across the cave. In anger, Gwiber filled the cave with fire. The intensity of the heat was too much for Skye's invisible barrier, wounded and burnt, she fled deeper into the cave.

Screaming in agony, Gwiber cauterised the wound with his own fire and hobbled after Skye.

~

Skye, her clothing smouldering and her body burnt, fell into the cave. 'I've done what I can,' she sobbed through her pain, 'but Gwiber is behind me.'

Staggering to his feet, Fin allowed Jenny to help him to reach the carving on the cave wall. Placing his hand on it, Fin concentrated, and his hand began to glow. Cries of pain and anger echoed around them, as Gwiber grew closer.

A harsh grating sound indicated that Fin had opened the hidden door and Jenny pushed them all through it and slammed it shut, behind them.

'I have you now,' cried Gwiber to the empty cave. Snarling, he filled the room with fire and then groaned with disappointment when he saw no dead bodies on the floor. 'I will find you,' he said, as he searched the cave network, 'You cannot escape me.'

~

Frightened to make a noise, they lay in silence behind the closed door. Unable to move Fin collapsed into Jenny's arms. Having found a small stream that ran through the floor of the cave,

Sparrow poured cold water, over Skye's burns. The cooling effect of the water helped Skye a little, but she could not help whimpering in pain.

'I'll be honest with you,' said Sparrow, 'these burns are bad, and we risk infection if they are not treated with a sterile solution fairly soon.'

'That was very brave of you,' said Jenny, 'We heard what you said to Gwiber. Was that true?'

'All of it,' replied Skye, 'including my tendency to lie.'

'Have you lied to us?' asked Sparrow as she poured more cold water on her burns.

'No,' said Skye grimacing in pain. 'There was nothing to lie about. But there is one thing that is worrying me...'

Looking up from stroking Fin's face, Jenny waited for Skye to continue.

'I have been to Ynys Enlli, Bardsey Island before,' she continued, 'my foster parents were quite religious and into ornithology.'

'Ornithology?' said Sparrow.

'Birdwatching,' replied Jenny.

'The island has been a place of pilgrimage for centuries,' she added, 'Its remoteness means that many have come here seeking peace, but people also come here because they believe it to be the burial site of King Arthur.'

'Why does that worry you?' asked Jenny.

'But don't you see,' said Skye, 'I am the Nimuë, and have the power to wake King Arthur.'

'Then I can set your mind at rest,' said Jenny, 'because I happen to know where King Arthur is sleeping...'

'How?'

'That's a story for another day,' replied Jenny, 'when we are far away from here.'

'Oh my goodness,' said a shocked Sparrow as she held Skye's hand, 'You are the Nimuë stone.' Pulling out the old paper, Sparrow said, 'Two parts of this poem are about you. "I saw the Nimuë standing in the fog." That was you when we first met you! In fact, I seem to remember calling you, Nimuë.'

'I remember,' replied Skye, 'I didn't know who you were, so I didn't confirm it.'

'Then I am fulfilling another part of the poem,' continued Sparrow, 'for I am holding, "the living stone in my hand."'

CHAPTER 15 - ABOUT TIME
(Llangwnadl)

'We can't stay here much longer,' said Jenny, 'Skye's burns need treatment and Fin is weak and powerless.'

'I've heard nothing for hours,' Sparrow said with an ear to the secret entrance, 'Do you think Gwiber has gone?'

'I doubt it,' replied Skye, 'I chopped one of his legs off. He'll be sitting in the dark waiting for us to appear and to take his revenge.'

'Gwiber obviously doesn't know about the passageway,' continued Sparrow, 'otherwise he'd have followed us. I'm going to try the door.'

'Okay,' replied Jenny, 'but be careful.'

Putting her body against the door, Sparrow pushed and twisted the mechanism that opened it. The door having been opened once, now moved freely and Sparrow opened it a crack and peeked through. Leaning against the far wall sat a one-armed man. Nursing the stump of his arm in his other hand, he stirred and sniffed the air. A glow of light flashed in his eyes, and he spun around trying to see in the darkness. As she watched, the man's appearance shimmered, and he morphed into a dragon. Gingerly, trying not to put weight on his wounded leg, he crept towards the entrance.

Gently, Sparrow tried to close the door, but it had stuck a small piece of stone and scratched the floor with a scraping noise. Instantly, fire poured around the edges of the door as Gwiber sought to destroy them. Dropping Fin's head from her lap, Jenny jumped and joined Sparrow in slamming the door shut. The door closed with a crack but the mechanism shattered.

'Ow,' cried Sparrow, 'the door is heating up.'

'We all have to move,' replied Jenny, 'Gwiber is trying to break through the door.'

Sitting up and rubbing his head from where it had hit the ground when Jenny had jumped up, Fin finally looked awake and conscious. Looking at Skye and her burns, Fin's face filled with horror, 'What's been happening?'

'Can you walk?' asked Jenny.

'I think so,' he replied.

'Good, because Sparrow and I are going to have to carry Skye.'

As carefully as they could, Jenny lifted Skye's arm around her shoulder as Sparrow raised the other. As gentle as they were, Skye still screamed in pain.

'Do you have any powers left?' Jenny asked Fin.

'A little,' he replied.

'Good because I can see in the dark with my hair,' continued Jenny, 'but you and Sparrow are going to need to see where we are going.

~

Holding Skye in his arms, Fin struggled to

remember their journey through the passageways. At first, they had travelled upwards, but then they had reached a spiral staircase cut into the stone, and they went down. On reflection, Fin had lost count of the number of steps they had descended. However, it was worse for Skye, and she fainted. Now a dead weight, Sparrow and Jenny, took turns of carrying the unconscious Skye over their shoulders.

'Her breathing is getting worse,' Sparrow said as she checked on Skye.

'Shock is setting in,' whispered Fin, 'if we don't do something soon, she could die.'

'What can we do?' asked Jenny, 'She's too heavy to carry any distance, and your powers are gone.'

'Can you get into my mind?' asked Fin.

'Probably.'

'And bring Sparrow and Skye with you?'

'I've no idea.'

'Will you try?'

Gathering around Skye, Jenny pulled Sparrow and Fin into a group hug and closed her eyes.

~

The sun shone brightly down on Fin, Jenny, Sparrow and Skye as they sat next to the lake at Ravenswood House. The birds sang in the trees and the bees buzzed their way around the summer flowers.

'Where are we?' asked Sparrow.

'This is Ravenswood House,' replied Fin, 'and our home.'

'How did we get here?' continued Sparrow.

'We are not really here at all,' he replied, 'but

Jenny has brought you to a happy place in mind.'

Looking around her, Sparrow glanced at the black and white Tudor House, that seemed top heavy and rickety, 'It looks creepy to me!'

'Tell me about it,' he laughed in reply.

A groan emitted from Skye's prostrate form.

'No time to waste,' said Fin, 'In the caves, my powers were exhausted, but here they are strong, especially when you are with me.'

Carefully, Fin lay down on the ground next to Skye and gently placed his hands on her shoulders. As Sparrow watched, she saw Fin assume the full power of the Phoenix and soon he was almost too bright to look at. Together, Fin and Skye rose up into the air, Fin's wings, surrounding and engulfing Skye. Suddenly, Fin screamed out in agony and pain, and they collapsed to the ground.

The first to sit up was Skye, her burns and cuts now healed. Then Jenny pulled Fin to his feet and kissed him.

'And breathe,' laughed Sparrow.

~

Opening her eyes, Sparrow thought for a second that she had been struck blind, but then Fin's globe of light lit up the cave. They were all there, but miraculously, Skye was standing up and smiling.

'It worked,' said Jenny.

'It did,' Fin replied, 'and because you were all part of it, Skye has been healed, and I have some of my strength back.

'What's that noise?' asked Skye. 'It sounds like someone is hitting the ground with a giant hammer. It's deeper than I remember,' she continued, 'but it reminds me of when I once watched a craftsman tap out a bronze plate, on an anvil with a metal hammer.'

'That noise you can hear,' replied Fin, 'is the sea crashing on the rocks above us.'

'Then where are we?'

'At a guess, we are under Bardsey Island,' he explained, 'and we have walked under the sea to get here.'

~

Breathless, they climbed the last few steps of a seemingly endless spiral staircase and reached a cave with the brightest light, Sparrow had ever seen filling it.

'Is that Gwiber?' she asked.

'Daylight,' replied Fin.

Now able to see clearly, they exited the passageway above another cave and dropped down from the ledge to the floor beneath.

'If you didn't know it was there,' said Jenny looking back up at the roof the cave, 'you would never know that passage was there.'

Walking out of the cave, they looked back across the channel to Aberdaron, where it seemed clouds were being formed from the land itself.

'I guess Gwiber is still trying to burn his way through,' said Jenny, 'Come on we need to find a way off this island.

Approaching a natural harbour, they looked down to see if any vessels were visiting, seeing none they headed for the small outhouse they could see by the rocky wall.

Having found food, water and more importantly, toilets they all felt a lot better.

'It's time,' blurted Jenny.

'Time for what?' asked Fin.

'No time,' she replied as she fiddled with her ring. 'I know how this works now. When we went back to Ravenswood House in your head, it all became clear.'

Interested, they all listened intently.

'I thought that all I needed to do was focus the power of the ring on when I wanted to be, and it would take me there,' she explained, 'But I was wrong, I don't focus on the ring's power, the ring focuses on mine.'

Slightly confused, Fin said, 'Well that sort of makes sense.'

'The ring cannot give me something that I don't have to start off with,' continued Jenny, 'and yes it exhausts me, just like you using your power exhausts you when you do something big and crazy!'

'Me?'

'Yes, you,' laughed Jenny, 'Come on group hug time!'

As Jenny wrapped her arms around her friends, she whispered, 'Hold tight.'

The world swirled around them as day became night, and the seasons and years flew past them.

Opening his eyes, Fin looked around him, 'Where and when are we?'

'Where is easy,' replied Jenny, 'we are in Llangwnadl, Porth Golmon to be precise. When is a different matter.'

'Wait,' cried Sparrow, as she ran over and picked up a newspaper that had been dropped on the path. 'We are back in our own time, it's the date we left to go back in time with Gwyneth.'

'That's fantastic,' said Fin.

However, their excitement instantly faded when they heard Gabriel's howl echo in the distance.

PUBLIC MEETING

SAVE OUR HISTORIC WELL

- Of great historical heritage
- Part of the pilgrims route to Bardsey Island.
- Closed off from the general public,
- denying pilgrims access to its miraculous "laughing Waters."
- We need your help to support its public reopening.'

'St Aelhaiarn's Well (Ffynnon Aelhaearn) has a great historical heritage, and despite being in all the guide books, has remained closed. Originally, it formed part of the pilgrims route through the Lleyn Peninsula on to Bardsey Island. In 1900, following a diphtheria outbreak, the well was closed off from the general public, denying pilgrims access to its miraculous "laughing Waters." We need your help to support its public reopening.'

HAVE YOUR SAY AND SHOW YOUR SUPPORT

WEDNESDAY 6PM

Llanaelhaearn Community Centre

CHAPTER 16 – THE LAUGHING WATER
(*Llanaelhaiarn*)

'How did he find us so quickly?' asked Fin.

Quietly, they meandered their way back into the town and got thoroughly lost. Finally, Fin indicated that they should take the main road to Nefyn, and reluctantly they followed the path. However, whichever route they chose they could hear Gabriel's howls in the distance.

'We need to find somewhere to hide,' said an exhausted Sparrow, 'I'm sorry, but I need to rest.'

Reaching what appeared to be a church, they stopped outside a small stone building that advertised itself as, 'St Aelhaearn's Well, Roofed 1900.'

'Maybe we can rest in here,' said Fin as he rattled the door.

'Why would you have a well inside an outhouse?' asked Jenny.

'No idea,' replied Fin, as he felt the large gate hinges and traditional bolt and padlock. Allowing his hands to glow, Fin pulled the lock apart in his hands and opened the door.

Slipping inside, Fin closed the door behind them

and tired, they sat on the stone bench. The water in the stone well reflected the light from the ventilation holes drilled into the door, and nobody wanted to risk drinking it. Picking up a leaflet that had been shoved under the door, Fin allowed his hands to glow and read it aloud to the others.

'St Aelhaiarn's Well (Ffynnon Aelhaearn) has a great historical heritage, and despite being in all the guidebooks, remains closed. Originally, it formed part of the pilgrim's route through the Lleyn Peninsula on to Bardsey Island. In 1900, following a diphtheria outbreak, the well was closed off from the general public, denying pilgrims access to its miraculous "laughing Waters." We need your help to support its public reopening.'

'Boring,' yawned Skye as she drifted off to sleep.

Despite, being cold and uncomfortable, all but Fin, fell asleep.

Unaware, that he had dozed off for a moment, Fin awoke with a start as he heard snuffling from outside the door.

'Where are they?' asked Gabriel, 'I caught their scent on the main road, but it has now vanished.'

'I have no idea, my Lord,' replied a second hound.

'These children are an enigma to me,' continued Gabriel, 'they seem to appear and disappear at will. They have appeared at different periods of my life, in what seems to me, to be in the wrong order.'

'They are our prey, Lord.'

'Indeed they are,' continued Gabriel, 'then where are they now?'

'Could they be in the church?'

'If they are, then they are beyond our reach,' he replied, 'you know as well as I do that they are invisible to us when on "holy ground."'

Unable to concentrate, Fin fought to stay awake as he heard Gabriel's voice disappear into the distance, 'Invisible when on holy ground,' was his last thought as he dropped off into a deep sleep.

~

'If we are ever going to get out of this mess then we need to be heading for Carnarvon,' said Jenny, aiming her frustration at Fin.

'I know,' he replied.

'Then why are we heading back towards Aberdaron?' she asked.

'Because Gabriel and the hunt are expecting us to head for Carnarvon,' he replied, 'and on foot, we are travelling too slowly.'

'But why all the way back to Aberdaron?'

'You know why,' continued Fin, 'When they discover we are not heading for Carnarvon, they will double back to Llanaelhaiarn or Llangwnadl. It doesn't make sense for us to go back to Aberdaron so they will not be expecting it.'

'Tell me about it,' muttered Jenny.

~

As dawn broke on the horizon, they entered Aberdaron and drifted through the fishing village. Stopping in the centre, Fin examined a notice board and pointed at the advert for bicycle hire.

'What do you think?' he asked.

'It says that we should have phoned first,' replied Jenny, 'It also says that we should bring a deposit and some proof of identity.'

'Then we are stuffed,' said Skye, 'because we look a mess, and never mind the deposit we don't have any money left at all.'

'I have some money,' said Sparrow, 'but not enough to hire four bikes.'

Unable to think of any other option they headed up the hill towards Uwchmynydd and took the first right, and stopped outside 1 Dolfor.

'I could do it,' said Jenny reluctantly, 'I could make them lend us the bikes.'

Turning Jenny around to face him, Fin looked her in the eyes and considered how tired she looked.

'No, you can't,' Fin said, 'you are too tired and weary.'

'But...'

'No, you know I'm right,' he continued, 'Yes you could make them hire the bikes to us, but not only is that unfair on them, but you will also use up all your reserves in doing it.'

Standing quietly to one side, Sparrow agreed with Fin, 'I hate to admit it,' she said, 'but Fin's is right. We don't know what we are going to have to face ahead of us and you will need all the strength you have before this over.'

'Why don't we just get the bus?' asked Skye.

~

Gathering outside the Post Office, they enquired how much it would cost to travel directly to Carnarvon. Sparrow emptied out her tiny wallet, and they groaned in frustration.

'There's enough for two of us,' said Sparrow, 'but we are quite a lot short.'

Frustrated, they sat down outside a small shop and contemplated what they could do next.

'Here eat this,' said Sparrow, as she handed to each of them a stuffed baguette and a drink. Talking over any objections, she said, 'We couldn't afford the bus fare before and now we still can't, but at least we will have eaten something.'

'Thank you,' said Jenny as she took a large bite out of her baguette, 'we all needed to eat.'

Silence fell, and the only attention that they gained while they were eating was from a passing seagull, which disappeared after Fin threw a tiny ball of flame at it.

'Do that again,' said Jenny.

'Mmm,' replied Fin.

'Throw small balls of fire into the air,' she said.

Not sure what Jenny was talking about, Fin threw small balls of fire into the air.

'Perfect,' said Jenny, 'I have an idea.'

~

'Roll up, roll up,' cried Sparrow, 'Come and see the boy that can throw fire and the girl that can hypnotise you into doing amazing things.'

At first, a few tourists stopped and gave them pennies, but soon Fin's fire tricks gathered a larger crowd. However, it was Jenny that caught everyone's imagination, for with one look she had people juggling, standing on their heads doing things they had never done before.'

'You hate cigarettes,' she said to one man, following his wife's request, and immediately spitting out his cigarette he threw the remaining packet into the bin.

'Thank you,' said the lady, as she slipped Jenny two twenty-pound notes, 'You have made my day.'

Soon Sparrow and Skye had collected more than enough money to pay for their bus tickets to Carnarvon.

'Time to stop,' said Skye, 'we are gaining too much attention.'

Across the road, a passing police car stopped, and the driver wound down his window to see what was going on. But before the driver could say anything, they picked up their stuff from the floor and disappeared into the Post Office.

Once the Police car had moved on, Sparrow counted out their money to make sure that they had the exact fare needed for the bus. Jumping on the next bus, they settled down on the back seat, and looking out of the window they failed to see Gabriel standing at the bus stop.

CHAPTER 17 - THE EAGLE HOTEL
(Carnarvon)

The bus trundled along on the road and in no time at all they were all fast asleep. Outside the bus, watching shadows flew overhead, following and waiting.

Awaking with a start, Fin jumped when the bus driver yelled, 'Pwllheli, Bus Station, all change!'

Climbing off the vehicle, they gathered together in a corner and waited for their second bus to arrive. Overhead, the sky turned dark and ominous, and rain began to fall.

'I don't like it,' said Jenny, 'I can sense we are being watched.'

Peeking out through the dirty window, Fin looked all around them. On every post and gate sat a large, black crow. Unnerved by all the birds, passers-by would try to move them by clapping their hands. Pigeons and magpies flew off whenever someone made a noise, but the crows ignored the sound and watched the bus station.

'They are the eyes and ears for Frân, their Lord Crow,' whispered Skye, 'The Crows have found us.'

'Then I'm staying here,' said Sparrow, 'they will

not attack us, while we are with the other passengers.'

The forty-minutes transfer time passed by slowly. When the bus finally wheezed its doors open, all the waiting passengers were delighted to get away from the attention of the crows. However, once the bus moved, the birds rose up into the air and followed the bus. Unnerved, the regular passengers glanced fearfully out of the windows and the driver, also distracted, narrowly avoided crashing the bus into a tree.

'We need to calm everyone down,' said Fin, 'their nervousness is acting like a magnet for the crows and distracting the driver.'

'I have an idea,' said Sparrow. Reaching deep into her pockets, she pulled out the Magician's Stone and offered it to Jenny. 'You can walk in peoples' minds, hold this stone up and try and let it focus on the passengers.'

Remembering that the Magician's Stone granted peace and enlightenment, Jenny held up the stone between her fingers and allowed her thoughts to rest on it. The rock became warm to her touch and began to emit steady blue light. As the light bounced off the interior walls of the bus and reflected back onto the passengers, they visibly relaxed. The sense of fear vanished from the bus, and they all felt better for it. Handing the stone back to Sparrow, the light disappeared, but the sense of unease did not return, and everyone relaxed.

Their senses dimmed, the crows continued to fly overhead and follow the bus. However, from the coast came another more considerable shadow, radiating so much anger and bitterness, that the crows flew high to avoid it. Swooping lower, Gwiber overtook the bus and landed at a bus stop. Transforming into a man, it waited until the bus came, flagged it down and jumped on. Sitting down behind the driver, Gwiber waved the stump of his arm cheerily in greeting to his fellow passengers.

'Bugger,' whispered Jenny, 'Not only do we have the crows following us, but Gwiber has just got on.'

'It's twenty years since we last saw him,' replied Skye, 'do you think he'll remember us?'

'You cut his bloody hand off,' said Fin, 'your face will be imprinted on his mind.'

'A girl can dream,' she laughed.

'Stop swearing,' whispered Jenny, 'it's gaining us unwanted attention.'

At the front of the bus, Gwiber opened a newspaper and began to read. Pausing only to turn the page, he ignored the friends in the back seat of the bus.

Taking turns to watch out of the window, they kept an eye on the crows and the other eye on Gwiber.

'What's that?' asked Sparrow, pointing at a shadow keeping pace with the bus.

'Nothing,' replied Skye, 'it's just the shadow of the bus.'

'No, it's not,' said Fin, 'it and a handful of other shadows are running along beside us. I'm afraid the Wild Hunt has caught up with us, and the biggest shadow is Gabriel, himself.'

In horror, as they ran, they watched the shadows

turn into wolves.

'Then we are trapped,' said Jenny, 'we have nowhere else to run. Will they attack us on the bus?'

'I don't think so,' replied Fin, 'they will wait until we are on our own.'

The bus stopped as it approached the outskirts of Carnarvon and old lady climbed on. Slipping, she crashed to the floor and hit her head on a chair. Gently, Gwiber helped her to a seat beside him and gave her a handkerchief to stem the flow of blood.

'Do we need an ambulance?' asked the driver.

'No, I'm fine,' replied the lady, 'thanks to this gentleman I am okay.'

'Hold tight please,' shouted the driver, and they were travelling again.

'Not to be callous,' said Jenny, 'but I was anxious that we would have had to get off the bus if the lady had needed an ambulance.'

Without further disturbance, the bus travelled through Carnarvon and reached the Eagle Hotel on Newbrough Street.

'This is it,' said Fin, 'we have to get off.'

Reluctantly, they climbed off the bus and crossed the road to the hotel.

'What now?' asked Skye.

'I've no idea,' replied Fin.

Gathering together in the triangle made from the roads in front of the Eagle Hotel they waited. An unnatural mist gathered around them and clung to the pedestrian railings. Overhead, the sky went dark, and they were surrounded by silently flying crows.

'Enough,' cried the Crow, and the birds landed on the railings.

A laughing figure emerged out of the mist and quickly transformed into Gwiber, the dragon. 'Do you like my mist,' he asked, 'it adds an air of mystery?'

Gathered together in a circle, Fin, Jenny, Sparrow and Skye, stood back to back.

The Crow bowed his head in respect to Gwiber and said, 'It has been a while.'

'Indeed,' replied Gwiber, 'and in different circumstances.'

Shadows emerged from the mist and surrounded Fin and his friends. Silently, the hounds of Gabriel gathered around them and in silence, sat down.'

'Why are they so quiet?' asked Skye.

'Did I not once tell you, that you need not fear them while they howl,' said the old lady, 'for they only howl when they are distant from their prey. It is when they go quiet that you are most at risk.'

'And now they are quiet,' acknowledged Fin. 'I wondered if that was you when you got the bus.'

'Who?' asked Skye and then answered her own question, 'Oh, Gwyneth.'

'So Gabriel, we meet again,' said Gwyneth, 'and I see that you have found your prey.'

'Indeed,' replied Gabriel, 'and it has been a long chase.'

'Then carry out your instructions,' screamed the Crow, 'for I grow tired and desire my prize, the Magician's Stone.'

'You will get your prize,' replied Gabriel, 'of that my Lord Annwn was certain.'

'Then kill the children and move on,' continued the Crow.

'And why would I do that?' asked Gabriel, 'For when I was in need, they rescued me, and when I was dying, they saved me.'

'What?'

'Therefore, they are no longer my prey.'

'Then who is?'

'You, my dear Crow!' continued Gabriel, 'You thought you could summon the Wild Hunt to commit murder for you.'

'Give me the Magician's Stone,' cried the Crow.

'The stone is of no consequence to me.'

'You serve me!'

'The Hounds of Gabriel serve no lying Crow!' said Gabriel and leapt.

In an instant, the Crow was gone and with him the watching birds. Lashing out in anger, Gwiber struck out at Gabriel with his remaining front claw and slashed the hound's neck. Gabriel fell to the ground in a pool of blood.

Before Fin could react, Gwyneth screamed, 'I am Gwyneth, Scylla, the last daughter of Ekhidna and the mother of all monsters. I play in time, for I am immortal and you have just killed an old friend of mine.' Wrapping her arms around Gwiber, Gwyneth allowed herself to age, and as she did so, Gwiber turned to dust.

EPILOGUE

Taking Gabriel in his arms, Fin picked him up and held his broken body to his chest. Ignoring Gabriel's whelps of pain Fin tried to turn into the Phoenix and heal him. However, the chase had left Fin exhausted and powerless, and he stumbled to his knees, whispering, 'I am so sorry.'

A figure appeared in the mist and waved his hand in the air. The Magician's Stone flew out of Sparrow's inner pocket, through the air and into Fin's hand. Immediately, the healing power of the stone revitalised Fin, and he transformed into the Phoenix and engulfed Gabriel in his fiery wings. Suddenly screaming in agony, Fin fell motionless to the ground and only awoke when Gabriel licked him.

With Gwiber gone, the mist cleared, and the passing traffic resumed. Struggling to his feet, Fin stood up to face the mysterious figure who had helped him. Before he could say anything, a figure ran past him.

'Reece,' cried Sparrow and flung herself into her friend's arms.

When Sparrow finally let go of Reece, Fin smiled

and said to him, 'Yours I believe,' and placed the blue gem into his hand.

'Thank you,' Reece replied and slipped the stone into his armlet.

'And this is...' began Sparrow, as she tried to introduce Skye to her friend.

'Nimuë,' he said, 'the living stone... daughter of...'

'Skye,' continued Sparrow, 'my new and trusted friend.'

'My pleasure to meet you,' said Reece, 'any friend of Sparrow's is a friend of mine.'

The door to the hotel swung open, and a very pregnant lady emerged, 'And where the hell did you get?' she asked, 'I let you go for a simple walk...'

'Elizabeth,' cried Fin and Jenny in unison.

FIN BUTLER IS ON FACEBOOK

Hi, my name is Fin Butler, and this book continues the story of my life. If you would like to chat with me, I would love to hear from you. Sadly, I have to sneak out of the grounds and go to a friend's house to access the page so I may be a bit slow in replying to you but I will try really hard.

www.facebook.com/FenixButler

ABOUT THE AUTHOR

Philip Janvier was born in Liverpool in 1957 and
studied Theology at Trinity College, Bristol. He is
addicted to reading, loves children's fantasy novels
and is the author of the 'Fin Butler' children's'
fantasy adventure series, he has written both
Christian and secular material including audio plays
and magazine articles. He is an award-winning
documentary videographer. He is married and lives
in Liverpool where he is the Team Rector of
St Stephen's, Gateacre.

www.ingramcontent.com/pod-product-compliance
Lightning Source LLC
Chambersburg PA
CBHW070342130626
46556CB00007B/2981